novum

AF192131

SANDRA SIEVERS

Untitled
a Book about
God and Creation
A Psychosis with Rhyme and Reason

novum pro

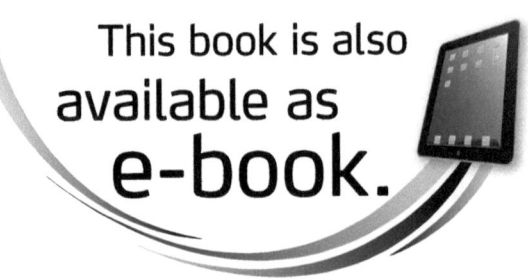

This book is also available as e-book.

www.novumpublishing.com

Preface

"Just be careful you don't get carried away with it all", was my sister's response to my idea of writing another book. My first book ended in a severe psychosis. So, I burned it, hoping the haunting would stop. But it did not, at least not yet.

I, too, am worried that things might become a bit strange again. That I might relapse. The writing process always comes with this subliminal fear.

However, this fear is deeply embedded in me anyway – whether or not I write a book.

Hopefully, the book will help me to no longer feel quite as alone with this horrible experience. I want other people to listen to what I have to say and read about my psychosis so that my feeling of loneliness may diminish, at least a bit.

Yes: illness will make you lonely.

My hope is that by writing this book I will be able to come to terms with my psychosis.

To write down all the memories one last time, to get them off my chest and to feel less alone with what happened – yes, that's my goal.

My first book was about one's own self, about being nobody and being someone (although I refer to myself as a nobody), the injustices in the world – in fact, the failure to understand that one thinks only in terms of national borders and does not see oneself as part of a global community. It also dealt with the superficiality of the life of a good old taxpayer.

Towards the end of the book, I tried to explain the world or how it came into being, and so the subject of God crept in. I began writing my first book as a non-believer, then evolved into a believer who was in touch with God, and ended up as someone who thought they were God.

Now I've become someone who jolts at utterances like "Thank God", "Oh God", "For God's sake", etc., because they always remind me of what's occurred.
I simply don't want to have anything more to do with the subject of God and Creation, hence this is my attempt to at least partially bring this topic to a close.

I overlooked some fractions of my first book when I burned, or rather, deleted it.
These are now attached as an appendix.

The Theory of Incidence and Expansion

in View of Double to Multiple Meanings and Possibilities

The world was not created by a Big Bang, but through an incidence: a first small nucleus that collapsed without destroying itself in the process – it expanded further and everything came into being.

The term "incidence" is to be understood ambiguously and in relation to its close cousin "incident": There has always been a consciousness (God), because without meaning and consciousness no incident would be possible at all. Thus, how science and religion are compatible with each other.

As humans, we are, in a sense, one big split personality. Everything is merely a multi-alternate possibility of the first nucleus – from plants to animals to human beings. So you don't need complicated formulas to understand the world or to explain it; everything can be explained by the expansion of the first small nucleus.

'Consciousness' has always existed, 'meaning' is existence/life/being.

Reincarnation or Wandering Souls

as Described by Jean Paul

Jean Paul assumed that there is a transmigration of souls.
The human body is merely a shell, the soul or the self is the core.
This theory also played a role in my psychosis/my experiences,
especially in the early days.

The Illusory World

and Good and Evil

In my book, I described our world as a make-believe, illusory world in which existence is not truly possible: each of us should feel guilty as we silently accept the wars and deaths caused by famine each and every day.

Moreover, the rules and norms of a community based on solidarity do not allow one to develop one's self or to live out one's self freely – anyone who is not a well-behaved taxpayer or average citizen is marginalized and ostracized.

Good and Evil exist, though Evil rules the world. After all, there are still wars being waged and property is unfairly distributed. I criticize the many believers, in particular, because they are the ones who ultimately always plead for the grace of charity.

The division into Good and Evil also played a role in my psychosis.

Further

Elucidations

In this book, I describe what I experienced as I perceived it in the respective situations; I didn't think I was crazy – at least not in the sense of an illness.

Mentally, I was, in fact, crazy: I existed in a real parallel world. "After all, scriptures like the Bible would not even exist without these kinds of parallel world experiences. In today's time, Jesus would probably also be declared crazy and sick," I wrote in a letter to a monastery.

I even wrote to the German Chancellor. Naturally, I did not receive a reply.

But I was sure: I'm not ill; I am in contact with God and the Beyond.

I also saw things online, on TV or on shows that others didn't see. I will explain these things later.

When it came to interpersonal matters, I also caught things that were not uttered at all in our world, that only I heard; perhaps that I had just imagined too.

It is still difficult for me to convince myself that none of this was real.

It just felt too real, and at the same time it was also the worst thing I've ever had to experience.

The Big Bang

Theory

It started with the series "The Big Bang Theory": Everyone was the ego, the self.

"So great to finally get to know you a little better", they'd say to each other and shake hands.

They'd make fun of string theory. Furthermore, two actors played a game with a long rope: "This far?" "Yes, this far" – "This far" is how far God is from us humans.

Radio station search

The following morning, I opened Instagram – again, everyone was the ego.

There was also a new brutal computer game in which everyone fought everyone else.

Because of this game, I was worried: people didn't seem to value life anymore, it was all simply the perpetual rebirth of the ego.

So, I rang up a university for physics: "Have you already heard that God has proved His existence?

I would like to show you what I've written on the subject."

It was a Saturday, and he was "the wrong person to talk to anyway."

And so I decided to go to a local radio station.

"What's this all about?" "It's about saving humanity," I answered.

Of course, they didn't pay any heed to me, and the boss wasn't there either, so I drove on to the Ruhr region, but they didn't find any time for me there either.

Disappointed, I drove back home.

Germany

seeks a Global Concept

"Deutschland sucht den Superstar" (German Idol) was on TV in the evening. Here, too, everyone was the I, the me, the ego. The jury was looking for a global concept or a slogan, basically a motto, though none of the candidates managed to impress them. Somehow, I felt spoken to, so I thought of a few phrases: "Faith in the good", "Sharing a task: life", "Inspiration."

Nothing really worked, German Idol continued to be strange and unchanged.

It all sort of frightened me, so I asked my (now ex) boyfriend whether I could come over. He said yes.

Karl

Lagerfeld

Before I got going, I checked my Instagram once more: It was full of Karl Lagerfeld, as he had just died.

Was he somehow connected to all these strange events?

I did some research and found out that about five months earlier he had contacted the music group Genetikk, who call themselves "young gods."

He also left behind the slogan "The beat goes on." That actually seemed to be the case; yes, I was sure that he was behind all of this.

Had he experienced something similar to me right before his death? Maybe he even became a god? Perhaps.

God

is great

Arriving at my boyfriend's house, I asked for a pen and some paper, as I had more ideas.

I wrote down equations such as "God = Love," but there was always an unfitting one such as "Sex = Greed." So there was always a variable that spoke against a world at peace.

Suddenly, fear came over me again: I had come too close to God. I wanted to burn my notes. My boyfriend finally took hold of them to throw them away.

"I don't feel at home here," he uttered out of nowhere, as we were lying next to each other.

The transmigration of souls? Who or what was speaking through him?

"So, feeling cold yet?" he asked. He was scaring me.

His smile was devilish; Evil seemed to be speaking through him.

"Please, let me continue to exist. I promise I'll make myself smaller and less conspicuous," is how I – the Good – had to implore him – the Evil.

He opened a window and I was convinced he'd call for help, so that Evil would ultimately be stronger and win.

I couldn't allow that to happen and so I rushed to the window, which shattered in the process.

"God is great!" I yelled from the window.

I was now sure of one thing: *That* must have been the phrase sought for earlier.

Day 1

The police

My boyfriend Ivan called the police. When they arrived, he said I had gone mad and told them what had happened. "Why are you bad-mouthing me?" I asked – after all, I was the innocent one, the Good.

The police asked me to go with them.

Outside, I yelled once more, "God is great!" – as a kind of cry for help.

There were two police officers: one good, the other bad.

"We need each other – the core and the shell – just like Good and Evil, we must not destroy each other completely," I said, appealing to their conscience.

Once at the precinct, the story continued in a similar fashion: there were both good and bad cops.

They wanted to put me in a solitary cell. I resisted and threw myself to the ground, holding on to a police officer's legs.

"I can't be by myself right now," I cried miserably and full of fear. In the end, they were merciful, and I was taken to an office where a police officer was waiting to question me.

"I am so sorry that I questioned everything and the world as it is; perhaps we do need appearances alongside what is real.

I just want to be permitted to continue to exist, I want to go home, and I wish everything would go back to normal," I said.

The police officers were discussing among themselves in the hallway.

So I got up and repeated again into the hallway, "We need each other, we can't completely destroy each other." "Now remain calm, you'll be fine – just let me handle this," said the police officer in the office.

He put in a word for me, so I was allowed to go back home. Though I wasn't permitted to drive myself, so my dad had to come pick me up.

"If you're one of the good ones, too, reach out to me," the police officer whispered to my dad in parting.

I looked into my father's eyes and could not say for sure whether he was Good or Evil.

Once at home, I encountered my mother. I recognized Evil in her eyes.

Full of dread and uncertainty, I lay down in my bed and tormented myself to sleep.

Day 2

Amends, the police and the psychologist

The next morning, I knocked on my sister's door.

I hadn't seen her again yesterday. Was she Good or Evil? Or had Evil harmed her perhaps? She didn't open the door despite my loud and repeated knocking.

I was very worried about her, so I went and got my parents.

We finally managed to wake her. She then opened the door and appeared quite exhausted, but luckily, she didn't seem to be Evil. A bit later, I asked my dad to drive me to the next town to go pick up my car. He said yes. We talked a bit during the drive.

"If your TV's on the fritz, you'll have to send it in," he suggested. "But it's Sunday, what am I going to do with my TV? Put it in the basement?" I asked.

He didn't reply. Once we got to my car he said, "You can't just take all the time."

What did he mean by that? Should I apologize to my boyfriend for last night?

"Go ahead and drive home, I have something I need to sort out," I said to him and walked to my boyfriend's apartment. We hugged when he opened the door.

"I'm sorry about the window," I said. "Oh, it's fine," he replied. Everything seemed to be OK.

"What should I do with my TV? Put it in the basement?" I asked. "Maybe that would be best," he said.

"Let's go take a walk," he suggested. We strolled through town arm in arm.

Dusk slowly began to fall and with the growing darkness things became strange again:

"I love you," I said. He replied, "I love Ivan and Ivan loves me, but I also like you." And there it was: that devilish grin.

"Why do you want to destroy me?" I asked. "Come on, let's go home," he said.

I was very afraid again. *What's his plan?* I wondered.

When we got to the apartment door we bumped into a neighbor. We shook hands and he introduced himself. He wanted to keep talking but Ivan said, "We're going to head inside, see you!"

"He's one of the good ones too," Ivan then said to me. He smiled that devilish smile again.

So that is why he had wanted to keep things brief.

Once in the apartment, I began to cry. "Why are you doing this? Why do you treat me this way?"

Then suddenly, my best friend texted me, "Where are you? Come on over, I'm at home."

My savior, I thought. "I'm going to drive home," I said to him.

"Well, drive safe and don't think of anything but the road on your way home," he replied.

Was my Ivan speaking through him? Was he trying to protect me from Evil? Yes – is what I thought.

So I drove to my best friend's house.

"The road – a path," I kept repeating to myself during the drive and forced myself not to think of anything else.

Once I arrived, I texted her that I was there and asked her whether I should come in.

"I'll be right out," she replied. I was therefore not allowed to enter her domain.

She opened the door and I fell into her arms. I began to weep, "I am so sorry."

"That's all right," she said, giving me a motherly hug – she was one of the good ones. Was God speaking through her?
Perhaps.

"C'mon, let's go for a walk and you can tell me what's happened in peace and quiet," she suggested. "Ivan wrote to me asking whether I made it home. What should I do? Reply? And if I do, what do I write?" I asked, unsure.

"Don't sweat it, leave your phone in the car. You can answer later," she replied.

So we went for a stroll and finally sat down on a bench.

I told her everything. "I really don't know anything about this. I'm just going to make a quick phone call," she said, taking a few steps back. A little while later she came back and said, "Someone will be here soon to help us. Don't be scared."

"Okay," I replied – trusting her.

A few minutes later, a big van pulled up: the cops – here to serve and protect.

Two officers got out, one talked to me, the other to her.

I told them about the content of my book and what had happened the past few days.

"We're not familiar with that either," the police said.

"Perhaps I can talk to a psychologist," I suggested myself as the last possible solution.

After all, it was about psychology: the transmigration of souls, the subconscious, one's own self. "However, if I am right with my theory of the illusory world, even a psychologist won't be able to help me," I warned.

And I was to be proved right.

Arriving at the psychiatric clinic, I had uttered but two sentences before the psychologist said: "That's an acute psychosis! You have to stay here!" In his eyes I saw Evil and at the same time great suffering. "You see? I was right. I don't want to stay here, please help me," I said to the police. In the end, I did have to stay.

"I can see the suffering in your eyes, I too have suffered much. I'm not only Good – I am both Good and Evil. Please do not think of me as your enemy. Something is speaking through me – we must not destroy each other," I said.

Suddenly I saw fear or rather reverence in the psychologist's eyes. "So you're both?" he asked. "Yes," I replied.

In that way, I was also a bit like him.

Nevertheless, I was still worried; they wanted to give me a pill, which I initially refused, worried they wanted to eliminate me as the Good.

After further discussion, I took it anyway and stayed in the psych ward.

Shortly thereafter, I went into the smoking room to have a cigarette.

The people in the room looked at me curiously, almost voraciously.

I recognized Evil and greed in their eyes – I felt like I was the only good one far and wide.

"Can I braid your hair?" an older woman asked me.

Despite or because of my fear, I agreed; better not to reject her.

My fear appeared to be unfounded – the braiding was a painless undertaking.

A young man left the room and returned a little later.

He was wearing a new sweatshirt that said "I have a solution, but it doesn't fit the problem."

Somehow, I felt it spoke to me and yes: I did not have a suitable solution.

That night, too, I struggled to fall asleep, the feeling of fear and uncertainty not letting go of me.

The newspaper

Meanwhile I was in the open ward.
I went outside for a smoke.
Once there, I saw a stack of newspapers.
I glanced at the cover: "What Man Really Is," "A Conversation Between Man and Woman," "Cars Should Be Abolished" were the titles on the first page.
I went back upstairs and asked the nursing staff if I could bring the paper in.
"Yes, go right ahead," a nurse replied.
When I picked up the newspaper, I was startled: the titles were now completely different.
I was annoyed that I had not taken a picture.

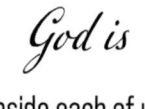

God is

inside each of us

I walked down the hall and told as many people as I could, "God is in each of us because He wants to live, but I just want to remain Sandra – with my family and friends." I also adopted this statement as my WhatsApp status.

In a way, I had to serve God; He would come to all the people to whom I made the above statement.

It struck me after some time: I wasn't permitted to say it to too many people, because otherwise very many selves would be lost and the world would be on this side as it is in the hereafter: Everyone would be the "I", the ego. I was deeply distressed and didn't know what to do, so I finally lay down in bed.

The sin

Suddenly my lighter was gone. The contacts in my phone kept deleting and adding as if by themselves. I was certain: God was behind this.
Was smoking a sin? Should I refrain from smoking?
I couldn't because my addiction was too great.
I also found enough arguments or excuses online assuring me that smoking is not a sin.
Outside, I asked a young man for a lighter.
"Here, you can keep it," he said, holding out a lighter to me.
A little later he told me that he had stolen the lighter.
I felt really awful – I had sinned by possessing a stolen lighter.
And yet I had not known about this theft, so I hoped for mercy.
I gave the lighter back to him.
"Will you come to my room? I want to show you something," said the young man.
I don't remember what he showed me, only what he said: "You know that we have to do it now?" he asked.
"No, we don't," I replied.
It felt like we were Adam and Eve who had committed sin together – the stolen lighter was the forbidden fruit.

God speaks

through everything

I was sitting outside smoking a cigarette. There were a few other people sitting next to me.

An older man said out of nowhere, "Man in himself is not evil, it depends on how and whether he acts." He voiced my original thoughts of the first book without me having ever shared these with him. Full of dread, I ran to the chapel.

There I opened a prayer book and read: "God speaks through everything."

Had I now become God? Was my mind expanding?

In my head I sensed discomfort, a feeling as if my brain was electrified – yes, a feeling as if my mind was actually expanding.

Another man said, "Sometimes I feel like I've lived before." – Did he subconsciously know about the perpetual rebirth of the ego?

All of this scared me. I went up to my room and knew exactly what to do or write down: "I don't want to be certain about God, I just want to believe. May the world, the people and everything remain sublime."

I then tore up the note and threw it in the trash so I wouldn't remember it later.

Yet I still perceived these discomforts.

When Jesus was alive there was an earthquake. I was sure this earthquake came about because he also wrote down those very lines. There was an earthquake and a change in his brain: he no longer knew for sure, only believed. Hence also the belief in (not: knowledge of) God.

So, after his rebirth he was probably "dumb."

Would the same thing happen to me? I would have put up with it, because all I wanted was for this nightmare to finally end.

Unfortunately, nothing happened except for a few strange statements from other people (the woman I was sharing a room with, using a devilish voice when I threw the note into the trash: "Well, have we done our duty again?"). Outside, a strong wind was raging.

The burning
of the book

By now I was certain: There is no Good or Evil. You are always both.

God is also both; no one is free from sin. Everything is the same: Good and Evil and the ego.

Because of all the bad experiences, I decided to burn my book. So, I drove back home and took everything I had written outside to set fire to it on the patio.

A strong wind had come up in the meantime. It was almost as if the world would end at any moment.

After burning my notes, I decisively grabbed my phone and entered a new status for my WhatsApp: "No matter who or what I am: My kingdom come, my will be done."

I then got in my car to drive back to the clinic.

"My kingdom come. It will be – as described in books – a paradise, every person, every soul will be alive here again, everyone will meet their loved ones again," I said during the drive. Clouds appeared in the sky in the shape of a heart.

"My kingdom come – NOW!" But as always, nothing happened.

"Must I die for love?" I asked myself.

In my first book, I wrote, "I would die for love, never for hate." I experienced a physical sense of discomfort again; a feeling like falling forever or vanishing into thin air.

"But I can't die, I am everything," I said.

Confused and desperate, I arrived at the clinic, where they were already waiting for me.

I am no one and everything – the concept of a world, but nobody must know about the concept, otherwise a world would

27

not function. There is no Heaven – no Paradise. Heaven is here on Earth and history repeats itself again and again: the perpetual rebirth of the ego. Hell is where God dwells; after all, He is alone and elsewhere, He cannot live or be with us.

"Thank you," said a young man with a devilish smile.

He was grateful that I had sacrificed myself to be God.

I was suddenly afraid of dying. So I approached the nursing staff and asked to be taken to the hospital.

Of course, they didn't take me seriously and naturally, once again nothing happened.

Catholics believe

in a reunion

My thoughts turned to God and Creation again.

Well, I am God, so I will wait for you and soon we will all meet again,
I thought. At the same moment, someone on the program
"Zwischen Tüll und Tränen" said, "Catholics believe in a reunion."
It kept happening that the TV expressed precisely what I was
thinking, but I can't remember much of it, or only vaguely.

There is no feeling worse than that.

You feel infinitely alone, yet it is you who speaks through everything.

On another occasion, I was in a supermarket and thought:
I guess I'll have to accept it then; I've become God, and suddenly "I'll
be the one" was playing on the radio.

Obsessive thoughts

and Earth's rotation

Humans are demigods, God and humans are meant to be kept apart, and other thoughts kept orbiting in my mind.

The Bible says something similar – but in a different, less cruel way.

Humankind thinks that God and man should be separate from each other – it is not God who separated us, but the thoughts of a person who thought they were God. Yes, I was sure: Jesus experienced the same thing in his time.

I even thought that the world rotates through our obsessive thoughts.

"I want to be dumb," I noted.

Suddenly, the commercials on TV had changed.

It was the disclaimer "Ask your doctor or pharmacist about risks and side effects," but what was shown was a jumble of letters like "nhjdkdf fjdf jksf jssjkfehfuehfu fedefed".

So, I had become God. Anything I wanted would occur everywhere.

"I want to be dead," I wrote down, but destroyed the note again.

Once again, I didn't know what to do and was falling into deep despair.

I picked up a piece of paper and pen and wrote down my last will and testament: "After I die, I want to be Sandra and without faith again.

I want my family to remain who they are today. I don't want to know or hear anything about God."

A few days later I was again so desperate that I wrote, "I want God's last will to be done. If that is not possible, I want to be dead."

Once again, I threw the note in the trash and lay down in bed. And again, I had this sense of unease.

So now I would become a non-believer and thus perhaps (nearly) brain dead. I would have accepted that, since I just wanted this horror to finally come to a close.

I stood up and picked the piece of paper out of the trash, striking the phrase "I want to be dead."

As always, nothing happened. I lay in my bed crying and tormented myself to sleep.

The love

and subconsciousness of a mother

My mother came to visit.
We went into town together and sat on a bench.
"Mom, I think I'm going to die because I've understood every-
thing," I told her.
"How do you send a heart on WhatsApp again?
Oh, I don't even know where that suddenly came from," she said.

Love

is a lie

I thought about everything again: the Theory of the Incident and Inception, the Rebirth of the Self, and so on.

Life is one incident: the collapse and inception of the first small nucleus.

After our death, at least dust remains – many small nuclei.

Is life, then, the collapse or the idea of death?

Is there any love at all in a world in which there is no "You", but only the "I"?

Suddenly I felt infinitely lonely and sad.

A while later, I met up with my best friend to do a little shopping. "I feel so dead," she uttered. Of course, she just meant that she was exhausted, but the choice of words made me shudder – it seemed to be speaking through her as well.

Not long after, songs like "Back to the start" by Michael Schulte or "Vermissen" by Juju came out. It seemed to be speaking through everything.

It seemed to me like they were only playing love songs on the radio. Everything was about love and the you – because I was afraid of losing everything (the you and love).

The ambiguous incident

and inception of a "We-World" with rhyme and reason

The world was created through an incident and an inception: a first small nucleus that collapsed in on itself in an incident without destroying itself.

On the contrary – it expanded and everything came into being. The word "incident" has a close cousin, namely "inception". The world was the result of an incident, i.e. the inception of a consciousness.

The inspiration: I want to exist. To be. Life. And above all: not to be alone.

So, a consciousness *(God?)* has always existed, because without rhyme and reason nothing would be possible at all.

This would make religion and science compatible.

Humanity and all of life is one big split personality.

Not being alone succeeds through the constant rebirth of the self, the ego.

Many people report a near-death experience in which they saw "a light."

So you see the light of day again and again without being able to remember your previous lives.

Strictly speaking, the ego lives alone in this world and deceives itself in order not to have to be alone or at least not to feel alone.

The first small kernel of consciousness *(God?)* wanted to live. And that's precisely what it accomplished: eternal life.

It lives in its own paradise – not alone, in a beautiful place called Earth, in the shell of a body, to be able to be and to act – to live.

The ability to forget is the key to perpetual rebirth, after which one does not remember one's previous life.

Only in this way is life in the here and now – life as 'We' – possible.

No one is free from sin because the first little kernel of consciousness wasn't either.

There is both Good and Evil in the world, as the first nucleus had both within it.

So are the wars and all the suffering in this world preordained?

Is a life now worth less, since it is merely the reborn ego?

Are God and the Devil a single entity that resides in all of us?

Why does the "I", the ego, which wants to live in the peaceful "We", kill?

Is compassion nothing more than self-pity?

Many questions arise from the Theory of Incident and Inception, which no one seems to be able to answer clearly, because none of us remembers when we were a small nucleus, let alone previous lives. But the fact remains: life is a miracle.

Every life, every human being has a dignity that must not be violated.

For we want but one thing: to be ourselves.

Jean Paul (* March 21, 1763 in Wunsiedel; † November 14, 1825 in Bayreuth) already assumed a transmigration of souls.

Perhaps life and death are just that: The wandering of the soul that wants to live in the "We."

Everything is but one of many "multiple possibilities" of the first nucleus – from the plant to the animal to the human being; everything carries the information of the first small nucleus within itself.

So you don't need complicated formulas to understand the world or to explain it; everything can be explained by the expansion of the first small nucleus that wanted to live (the kindred ideas of incident and inception).

The eternal
universe

The world was created by the incident and inception of a first small nucleus.
After death, many small nuclei remain.
After death, therefore, new things (life) come into being.
It is an everlasting cycle, without a beginning or end.
There are small universes, which together form a large whole, an infinite universe.

If there was a beginning, the beginning would be death (that is, a first small nucleus), but before death comes life.
Thus, life is more likely to be the beginning, but where did the first nucleus come from?
It was caused by a previous death.
So then is "nothingness" (the beginning of the universe according to many physicists) the same as death?
No, death is not nothing, it is an accumulation of nuclei and at the same time an indication of previous life.
But what is nothingness?
Is there or was there a nothingness at all?

In the field of physics, it is partly described as a certain energy, certain circumstances for being as a result, that was already present in the nothingness.
Is this energy life?
After all, no nucleus arises from life, but only from death.
So, does energy then result from life?
Is life the precondition for death? Yes.

Is death/the existence of nothingness the precondition for life/ being? Yes.

Thus, the beginning would be death/nothingness/the nucleus. But where does nothingness/death/the nucleus come from? Nothing can exist only where "something" once did. Death can only exist where there was once life/being. The nucleus can only exist where life and death once were. Is life the beginning/nothingness? Life is the precondition for death (see above). Life is also an indication of preceding something, because how could life arise from nothing? So there was some kind of energy. What is this energy? Is it death/the first nucleus after all? But where there is death, there once was life ...

Is there such a thing as eternal life? A life that already existed in the beginning? Or a life, which arises again and again (due to many deaths of universes) – so just an eternal life?

Is life energy and death nothingness? So an energy-charged nothingness is eternity?

However, death is not nothingness, it is at least a nucleus. Is life/being the energy-rich nothingness, and death the something? We can't really grasp life/being because we don't know much about its origin. Death on the other hand is tangible because life is its origin. So is there merely the origin of life? And thus, does life stand at the beginning? But where does life come from?

The question of whether death (the nucleus) or life (the being, the something in the nothingness) stood at the beginning thus cannot be answered clearly.

Hence the universe appears to be infinite.

Can eternity be equated with nothingness?
Neither is tangible or measurable.
So, is physics correct when it says that everything has its origin in nothingness?
Perhaps.

Eternity/nothingness is the answer to the question of what existed first. Nothingness existed and yet everything, life and death are in constant flux.
When observed from one specific point in time, nothingness is infinite, eternity is nothing.

Does God exist?
The first small nucleus collapsed and everything came into being. Just like that? Unlikely.
The first collapse, this incident must also be seen with its coupled word: inception.
The world was the result of an incident, i.e. the inception of a consciousness.
So, consciousness is also eternal.
Or is it perhaps this consciousness that marked the beginning/energy in nothingness?
Has there been consciousness since the first second of the universe?
How else could such a meaningful universe come into being, in which life/being is also possible?
By pure chance? Were we just lucky?
And how did it come to be that there is not just one living being or just one human being?
Where does the counterpart come from? Why does it exist?
Because someone had the desire/idea that there should be a we/us?
Why are there stars and other planets?
Because someone wanted us to have an environment to discover?
Or is it the self-interest of a consciousness that did not want to be alone?

A mind that longed for love and closeness?

Is this spirit reborn over and over again?

Was the Big Bang the idea and inception of the first little nucleus of consciousness, as it was finally no longer alone?

An inception that enabled eternal life in a paradise?

So, are the transcripts in the Bible to be interpreted differently?

Are we already living in Paradise without truly knowing it or without recognizing the world for what it is?

After all, wars are still being waged, people still experience famine, poverty and suffering.

Perhaps it is even our task to recognize the world as a paradise and accordingly live a life full of love and charity?

What comes after death, if it is not Paradise?

It is Paradise. We are perpetually born back into it to keep trying to do our job.

What happens when the task is done one day?

Will our sun then extinguish?

Will we be reborn in a different universe and everything will start all over again?

Is our destiny eternal life in the eternal pursuit of love?

"My-Works"

It appears *(not: seems)* to me most sensible to begin with the accumulation of smaller and larger "My-Works", which were probably *(as I wasn't aware of myself at this point)* the beginning of a journey; the beginning of my search.

This not-yet-conscious is, in my opinion, the interesting thing about it, since I have the following questions because of it:

Did my subconscious mind from the recent past already know about this journey that was beginning – the writing of my own, complete work? Does the subconsciousness determine the future? My own after-the-fact discovery doesn't allow me to come to any other conclusion. So, my answer is yes.

Do internal and external influences impact us equally?
Did the internal become the internal through the external?
Does the internal repeatedly change because of the external?
Does one go through several personalities in one's life?

Provided that the inside can be changed by external influences – absolutely.
Provided that the inside has a need to change – absolutely.

Is the social compulsion to live the one and only socially accepted life also of greater significance? Certainly: It probably either leads (subconsciously?) to the loss of the self in order to be able/allowed to remain part of this society, or it ultimately leads to the unleashing of the self in order to soon be oneself again.

To the extent that science or psychology says otherwise, did I ask for an opinion? – No. I am merely exploring my own psyche to make this my own science.
That's what I want: to create knowledge for myself about a (my)self.

Perhaps I would like to create a new global movement on the side. Who knows? (Who, if not us?)

So, I start with **My-Works from the recent past**, which at the same time probably marked the first step of a search for something in nothingness.
Most pieces, either in verbal and/or written form, are on my cell phone that serve me as a medium.

For your information, I started writing this My-Works roughly in late January 2019. ("2020 Project?")

I already wrote the ending relatively early in my writing process (acting).

This brings us to the selected self-reflections and My-Works from the recent past:
(11.2018 up to and including 01.21.2019 (day of the first audible call for help))

All works in this book are protected by copyright. I have just decided this myself, without knowing anything about it. What is mine is mine. You need to ask first. However, a lawful right must be in place where manners and decency are lacking. Human rights also apply to me, by the way. So please comply with these from now on.
Thank you despite it being a matter of course.

11.03.2018

The unrealized idea of one or more photos

1 field of flowers
1 meadow with a vase of flowers placed on it
1 meadow with a photo of a flower vase placed on it
1 meadow with a mobile phone placed on it with a flower photo
1 meadow
1 grave with flowers
1 empty grave
1 small flower
1 shriveled flower
Weeds
1 bee on a flower
1 dead bee
1 bouquet of flowers in a vase on a mowed cornfield *(11.02.2018)*

11.03.2018

About books and stories

Never open a book only to shut it again without a bookmark.
May an open book would better have been kept shut forever.
Only the author knows the correct interpretation of their stories.

11.06.2018

The unrealized idea of a horror story
(voice recording)

Title "Reanimation" or similar
A young man was brought back to life after 40 minutes of anguish, the resuscitation was successful. On the one hand he considers himself lucky, on the other, he is unhappy, because the in-between world of spirits won't let him go, despite living in the here and now.

Spirits who also want to return to their bodies; back to life, but they can't, after all their body as a shell is long dead.
The spirits represent a failed reanimation, which failed merely because not enough time was taken, hope was given up too quickly. Nobody fought for their lives for a full 40 minutes.

The spirits can't return to their dead bodies, nor are they ready to leave this world to vanish into the afterlife.
They are trapped as spirits in this world, but their bodies are already six feet under.
The young man was part of this twilight world for 40 minutes, in which the spirits also contacted him. After all, he was one of them for 40 minutes.

And because of this short stay, during which his spirit became acquainted with other spirits, his spirit is still in contact with the spirits of the intermediate world.
His spirit, however, returned to its body and thus became part of the real world again.
But from then on, his real world also includes the twilight world as a parallel world.
Because of this, the spirits can still reach him.

Ending, alternative 1:

The man attempts suicide but is reanimated successfully once again. Again, the same doctor. Again, the doctor took the time needed to save his life.

Consequently, the man's spirit visited the intermediate world again, where, originally, he wished to remain. The goal was to reach the hereafter, because he could no longer stand being in a world that included the parallel world. But he saw his wife standing there, crying miserably, so he wanted to return to life. And so, the reanimation was successful once more.

Back in this world, the spirits of the parallel world continued to tell him their stories. Among others: A 40-year-old father who died in a motorcycle accident and therefore missed the birth of his child. His wife now lives by herself, full of sorrow by the child's side. He wanted to return to life, but the doctors took only 15 minutes to resuscitate him and then gave up. Now he still roams this world, occasionally visiting his wife and child, but he can hardly stand it, because as a spirit they can neither see nor perceive him. He also can't stand seeing his wife's tears, not being able to comfort her.

Addendum:

The first few days after his resuscitation, all he could hear was voices. He thought he was mentally ill, and so did his family and friends.

So, he started seeing a therapist, took medication, but he didn't get better. One day another spirit spoke to him, "Don't you remember me? We spoke for nearly 40 minutes. I'm Tommy. We talked about how I fell from a window.

If they had taken the time, I too could be a man with a family today." Suddenly, the man actually remembered this conversation and knew: He isn't ill after all. This parallel world does exist. But they'll never believe him, so he has to keep it secret.

The spirits never left him satisfied, so one day he went mad and suffered from a persecution mania that wasn't really a mania or delusion. In the end, he was forcibly committed to a psych ward.

There he was alone with himself and the spirits, tied to a bed. And still, the spirits continued to speak to him, showing him horrific things.

Had it been his choice, the man would have liked to kill himself. The restraints prevented him from doing so, however.

He just wanted to escape from this world with its parallel world. It frightened him.

He did not return to his real life after the reanimation in the first place. After all, anyone who has been to this intermediate world is haunted by it until their death.

Ending, alternative 2:

He remains in the psychiatric clinic forever and dies from the tormenting fear of the parallel world or from old age. However, his spirit does not reach the afterlife either, but remains trapped in the intermediate world. He wasn't prepared to leave yet.

Not before he was finally believed. But he can't go back in any case, given that his body has aged too much by now and is too weak to host a spirit any longer.

Ending, alternative 3:

He breaks out of the mental clinic in order to commit suicide.

A totally different ending:

The man's wife was pregnant. He kills himself.

The newborn child is born with the ability to contact the parallel world without having been there. It was inherited because the father had entered this world at one point.

"Happy ending": the father remains trapped in the parallel world forever, but at least he can communicate with his son.

Final scene: The father, as a spirit, plays with the child, the child perceives him as being real.

Child lying in a crib – father shakes a rattle – child laughs from the bottom of his heart, finally falls asleep smiling.

Alternatively, the reanimated man in the story is, in fact, a woman who was pregnant but ultimately killed herself out of despair. The child in her belly could be saved.

This child, too, has the ability to contact spirits in the intermediate world so it does not have to grow up without a mother, despite everything.

12.27.2018

quote by Ernest Scheckeltyn

"If you cannot win, learn to fly."

01.10.2019

Tree of Life without roots

I can't identify with my former life.
Nor can I identify with my own actions or my previous companions
and guides.
A feeling as if my Tree of Life is missing roots.
Who am I? What is my purpose here? Am I really here?

01.18.2019

The crying of a newborn

Why do babies cry so much? Are they the only ones who can recognize the cruelty of reality, because outside thoughts cannot influence them yet?
Had the child's subconscious mind been preparing for a different reality; looking forward to a world that isn't this one?
Does the child feel disappointment from the first second, even before they can form a clear, conscious thought?

01.18.2019

The suppressed desire to break free

In objective terms, my current situation is bad.
But then again, what is objective?
No one has ever understood the entire big picture.
No one sees the little things that are actually the really big things.
Why does no one *(but me)* want to break free?

01.18.2019

What's the point of all this?

Why am I sharing all this?
I want to point out the grievance that no one can change anyway, except for everyone together.
I do hope for a do-over *for the world.*
Yet instead I will most likely grow lonely in *my world.*
Does happiness solely exist in the presence of suffering?

01.18.2019

The beautiful habit of living a lie

I'll tell you how I'm doing.
Not for pity.
One just feels sorry for oneself,
for being, *(appearing)*, to be who and what one is,
even doubting the meaning of one's own existence
or finally starting to change everything.

Formerly: "the fatty"
These days: *"kinda nice"*
"No tits, but some ass, scarred body."
Dimmed lights – that'll work.
Scarred soul
Dimmed emotions – that'll work.

Unintentionally noticeable in the past,
intentionally inconspicuous today.
But something inside me, despite everything,
still wants to speak to others; to ask:
"Who's coming with me to break out of this place?"
"Over here, me!" –
Oh, hi there nobody.
So nice of you to keep me company, again.
You – that something inside me.

Every person has two faces.
Every person can be bought.
Every person lives their own lie,
draws other liars under their spell.

01.19.2019

A victim's reckoning?

I am an embodiment of the fact
that the victims of society
at its core, and its abyss,
essentially hold the power in their hands.

We are what makes living in a make-believe world possible in
the first place.
They covet us as a target and
we don't even flinch.
You're welcome!

The reward is to see what happened to them:
they became servants of this perverted world.
That's why I'm happy to do without the money.
After all, *no one* likes to be underpaid for their work.

I don't need fans, I don't need pity.
One just feels sorry for oneself.
Is this a victim's reckoning?
Perhaps.
Could it even be a war against Evil by using its own weapons?

01.19.2019

The cell phone (not: The vibrator ... or is it?)

It vibrates but does not speak.
Seems strange to me, but *(is)* often so close.
("Is" does not exist in illusions and appearances, so it is excluded).

The self possesses

meaning for eternity even without titles and time:

**The self has great stature. It has (its own) great stature –
regardless of body size or other "racial classification."
It is the only thing that distinguishes people from each other.
The one thing that makes people unique;
makes an individual person unique:
The power of singularity.**

Rules

aka prohibitions

Only the forbidding of some things makes these things into something forbidden.

A female referee in soccer can *serve (in the truest sense of the word)* as an example here. A match was not broadcast in a country on the Asian continent because of her.

To clarify in advance: "The woman" here merely functions as a representative for things that are natural and independent and are pushed by the environment or by the society/government/rules/norms into dependency –

powerless and without free will.

While she still possesses free will, unfortunately this is of little interest to the free will of a coercive community.

There are definitely people who find the sight of men in short sports shorts unattractive. *Does anyone ban a game/fun/existence because of it? No.*

Women are reduced to superficial dolls who, no matter what they do or don't do, attract sexual attention – seemingly solely because of their presence or, in their absence, solely because of their existence. A disruptive factor.

Men are the *human beings; the kings*, women are ... *well, women.*
Women who exist solely to satisfy base needs, not to be referees or lifeguards, perhaps.

That would clearly be too suggestive.

Why do people think this way? Who or what decided that athletic shorts are directly related to sexual arousal?

Things that are banned only become interesting when they are banned.
(cf. also the century-old novel "Bible": the forbidden fruit).

One (or men) must not develop sexually inclined thoughts because of a woman – certain shows are not aired to prevent these thoughts from developing, and ultimately to solidify these horrible thought processes in people's minds; to turn them into remote-controlled, influenced, greedy servants who, despite their servanthood, never receive what they once desired: love.

But at least you are still allowed to have sex.
Provided that the act happens in a dark room; in an obscure place, so that the forbidden thought is exclusively inherent in the dark room and never comes out into the open.

Much like the dark chamber in the heart of man, a place once created for something like love.
Sadly, the government was not asked for approval on this point, so the presence of love is simply forbidden and hatred is spread.
Sex and love have nothing (more) to do with each other, they are not (any longer) dependent on each other and have no other connection.

Lust is not (anymore) the desire for love, but the urge for self-satisfaction of one's own urges.
It is only what remains despite various influences, because it is indestructible: an instinct. The primal instinct of a mammal.

The outcome: reproduction.
The outcome that was once not an outcome, but a miracle.
Merely a mammal still appreciates this potential miracle:
not man, but the trope or figurative image that the stork presents. A fantasy creature.
A lie? No.
The truth under the cover of unreality, because in our illusory reality the (this) truth is not permitted.

The hateful governments and societies are too busy killing miracles anyway to recognize them for what they are.

Even if they were in a position to do so, they would deny it, just to secure their job *(their power)* – under no circumstances would they ever permit their very meaning of life *(spreading hatred)* to be replaced by a machine *(love)*.
That's something you fight for, day in, day out. Around the world. Even at night, under the cover of silence and darkness, in which the world's ignored calls are mere whispers.
Great job. We've all done a great job.
Crazy what such negligence is capable of.

Mankind is evolving ...
(I deliberately leave this sentence open-ended so that the governments and systems of this world – not I as a woman, a human being – can make a judgment about the nature of the development. They know everything, after all. The power that creates "scientific knowledge."
A science unto itself and no one else)

The effect of this ban on love: One (or man) lusts after women, not love.
One (man) no longer sees the woman as an equal human being, but as a sex toy.
The thoughts of *a* sick mind in a position of power shape the thoughts *of* society.
The situation is quite similar in *"Germany"**, just not *(anymore)* quite as brutal or highly motivated and committed: Anyone who does not call themselves a "taxpayer" is a bad person who is essentially useless to society.

---

* *the name of a country governed by people, which isn't a country, since it belongs to no one, in which I finally began to interpret the world: a "sh...-place /word" – an illusory place*

On the contrary – they want to get rid of them, or at least keep them down.

Punish them?

Women … *are punished,* **because** *they are women.*
Men … *are punished,* **provided** *they perceive a woman to be more than just an object.***

Foreigners …
Gays …
Believers …
Non-believers …
Scientists …
Journalists …
Neighbors …
Work colleagues …
Welfare recipients …
Pensioners …
Dreamers …
Free thinkers …

People?

Society's losers are punished because they have recognized the overarching big picture that's wrong and rejected it for their one and only life plan.

** *A "wimp" is still better than a "simp." Anyway. That is just my opinion, which I am fortunately allowed to express freely in industrialized countries thanks to freedom of speech (without having to die in return, unless you find out who and where I am – so I will write my will afterward, free from fear and full of love for love. Yes, I would die for love. Only for love, never for hate), but which ultimately cannot impact the influenced opinion of others. Being just a small nobody, I lack the power and standing. Unfortunately, you cannot buy a wake-up either. But perhaps I will be left a small place in a dream of a better world. Only no one is living the dream, they continue to sleep through it. Night after night, under the cover of silence and darkness, in which, unfortunately, Evil is also in power, lurking beneath the surface. Let's just continue to dream about big-ass cars.*

Man lives the punishment for the punishment of a punishment.
Man punishes himself for his greed by living only to crave what is forbidden.
However, greed cannot be prohibited, it has been part of humanity since the very first second.
No one can ban thoughts either.
At least that is what I thought.

But it seems that you can shape greed into bad intentions and hence ultimately into bad actions by creating nonsensical rules – by dehumanizing man; making his free will the will of Evil.

Apart from greed, people once possessed reason, which usually led to acting out certain cravings merely in thought, not in reality; to not act (in a way that harms others).

Replace reason with rules, laws and governments and there you have it: the self-destruction robot. The eternal, rebellious teen who craves the forbidden fruit; who would do anything for that fruit: from lying to murder – many roads lead to the wrong destination.
But at least you *have* a goal, a meaning in your remote-controlled life.
That is worth fighting for. Destroying for. Killing for. Hating for. Living death for.

The balancing act: to seem happy in the meantime, in order not to destroy the appearance that keeps us quasi-alive and makes destruction in our hidden form possible in the first place.
No, I completely agree that nobody should have the right to take away our meaning in life.

Women have *tits*.
Men have a *chest*.
The woman *is* the *man's vagina (the legendary rib)*
The man *has a penis (and/or/aka) a brain.*

That's plenty of preconceptions.
We should finally start to use our commonality in a meaning-ful way: *To have big balls (or ovaries), (heads up, dearest "Govern-ments & Co Ltd", what follows is a free lesson: "metaphor", or rath-er a "figure of speech" is what this insinuation is also gladly called synonymously).*

People once possessed a functional, independent brain.
A long, long time ago, when no one yet began to play God, merely because the latter could not be proved, and seize power to rule, much as Satan would probably do in Hell: *He punishes mankind for acting badly by turning them into even worse human beings and, by the way, gradually into animals – beings without any free will, let alone the ability to think for themselves, to doubt truths, to dis-cover the world or to love (women and other forms of being human).*

Perhaps men should always strap a large cage around their pri-vate parts right before they (are allowed to?) leave the house.
This dangling banana in the pants calls to women, yes, it upsets women that men offer themselves in such a way.
So please, dear government. Govern!
Turn humankind into a mistake unworthy of life and love.
Thank you so much for nothing(ness).
And no, dear heretics aka non-believers: this is not necessarily an allu-sion to wearing a headscarf, rather it is an allusion to the acceptance of coercion, which does not occur in the first place unless you let it happen.

PS:
We cannot (any longer) **excuse our behavior with the belief in the "personal" faith of a strange prophet**.
Faith entails belief in the goodness of people.
In our world, however, this possibility is ruled out. Man lives the life of a being that is controlled by its urges, because it is precise-ly this **erroneous belief** that drew us to this person.

Man, humankind, had a pretty lousy childhood and adolescence.

But we cannot excuse everything with the past either.

Shouldn't one gradually grow up, form one's own opinion, and be allowed to express it despite "non-freedom of speech" in certain parts of the world?

Shouldn't one grow up now and realize that the monster under our bed is nothing more than our own fear? A fantasy, a conceit that does not allow education (forming an opinion) and leads to the formation of a split social personality.
The hatred and killing in the world as our home are pushed away, repressed.
Life and love are ignored or not valued.
We may have unlearned it due to lack of repetition, but the skill does not disappear. It's just like riding a bike.
The first attempt (after a long period of time) usually still feels a bit unfamiliar and shaky, but with time and some practice we easily return to our best form.

How can you possibly cherish anything in a world full of misery?
Well, first, by taking pleasure in the fact that one has not yet died because of one's own or someone else's agony (man is first and foremost an egoist). And second, that finally humankind has started therapy in order to be able to feel joy again during one's own process in life.
Only waking up and appreciating things makes the next step possible.
We must *appreciate and cherish life, even when we don't want to.*
Life is the value. Existence is our value. It is the thing that defines us.
So we have to love ourselves for what we are: alive; (still) existing.
A big step for ***humankind*** *– for each of us.*
We can only accomplish that together.
In group therapy.
We are simultaneously our therapist and patient.
Only we can heal what we ourselves once injured or broke.
Provided that it can still be healed, or that we aren't untreatable or perhaps long since dead inside already.

Human beings were, are, and will remain egoists.
Everything is perceived subjectively.
Objectivity does not exist.
The illusion exists.
You need a peaceful environment to live a joyful life.
Although we are already in a bad way
(for now, some people can still consciously perceive this),
at least we are still better off than others.

Injustice never leads to happiness: egotistical charades for us, self-
less death for the rest.
Existence for all – this is what makes happiness possible.
The joy of a single selfish person.
Life.

You should be completely selfish
and finally see the context, the connections.
Deny this selfish realization,
that "everyone better do well
so that I can finally do well,"
and you will likely not deserve any happiness,
for what you will receive is merely
the illusion of happiness.

The inverse of that and
a look into the past
provide all the answers
to questions that no one asks.

To suppress those questions using fear tactics.
No doubt about it: This is truly selfish in the selfish sense –
it is truly stupidity.

But thank goodness:
We've got a brain.
It's a little spongy,
but it does have potential
to be more than just spongy.
"Invest, invest, invest" –
this principle has its raison d'être;
but it is applied in the wrong place.
Outwardly, rather than inwardly.
Only the powerful illusion can do that:
To invest something into something external.
Almost magical,
were it not so deeply tragic.
Almost magical,
if the result wouldn't just be
NOTHING.

A look into the future

the e-future

Man has always enjoyed playing God.
While some busy themselves believing in Him, others spend their time trying to embody Him.
Do believers worship Evil?

The bicycle came first.
The bicycle aids man in his activities: locomotion.
It is true that the bicycle makes it possible to move around more quickly, nevertheless, it requires you to use your body.
You need your own hands and feet in any (normal) case.

In the further course, the engine and thus the car were developed.
An even faster way to get around, your foot is only needed to push a pedal, your hands to steer and shift gears when need be.
But at least the person still needs to act.

And what is soon to come? *Self-driving cars.*
And after that? *Robots that replace humans.*
Robots that evolve their own intelligence to ultimately destroy humans?
One thing a robot will probably never be able to feel: emotions.
Remorse, empathy, happiness, love, anger …
They destroy "by mistake" – *unlike humans.*

The intelligence of man, the urge of man to evolve, leads to the loss of human intelligence.
This is where Artificial Intelligence will soon step in.
Just as driverless cars will take over locomotion in the near future, Artificial Intelligence will soon take over thinking.

The result: thinking without feeling.

Or has man himself long since become the robot, the Artificial Intelligence?
Who even cares that for our money, people have to suffer and starve on the other side of the world? Nobody. We tune it all out.
Feelings are suppressed, illusions and appearances are lived.
Is the (illusory) human a robot?

A further development must somehow, somewhere, sometime have an end, otherwise this evolution becomes our own demise; otherwise, we are *not digging our own*, but *the* grave of humankind.
At this inappropriate point, of course, I don't want to leave out the important "environmental policies":
Who cares about the environment when the world is already drowning in trash?
Probably just the compulsive hoarders among the "environmentalists".
(Don't get me wrong: environment is important, but is this a reason/argument for ignoring things like hunger or war?)

Back to the first-and-only-world topic:
So, shouldn't a "normal car" be perfectly adequate?
Shouldn't we leave it at that?
We live in order to act. We act in order to live.
But soon the progressive, commendable digitalization will take over our acting, and shortly thereafter probably also thinking – the origin of every action.
You learn through acting again and again.
Learning simply *is* acting repeatedly.
Are people incorrigible?
Repeating an error is more than a straight "F" in school.
It is intentional. Bad intent.
(The "normal car" in this context is representative for technologies that do *not* completely replace man – his craft/action/existence/meaning).

Humankind is celebrating itself for developing the first human-like robots.

Many ordinary people already clean their homes either by using a robot vacuum or they hire a cleaner. At least in the case of the cleaner, you transfer the action to another person, even if it is for money, but at least the action (existence) as such is not completely lost. In the long run, however, "employing" a robot vacuum cleaner is more cost-effective and efficient.

The fact that we are ultimately destroying ourselves ... and *that* isn't a minor side effect, it's just that no one *"gives a shit"*.

Sorry, I forgot:

That *poor little ordinary person* has to work so hard that he can't keep his own home, the inside of his home *(also: his self) clean* by himself. He *doesn't have* the time.

Who really says *what's necessary* and *what is not*?

You, yourself? The boss? The system? The money? Evil?

Who is living *that single*, unique *life* that we know? *You? The boss? ...*

Evil.

A few fun questions for the circle of believers:

What was God's plan? Humanity's own self-destruction?

Not being human, not being who you are?

Is life the bill for having tasted the poisonous fruit we craved?

– End of the fun questions –

Shouldn't Artificial Intelligence only be developed *as far* as is factually necessary? For example, for people with disabilities who are limited in their agency.

Shouldn't these kind of people benefit from further developments? *Shouldn't the creation of an artificial intelligence merely support rather than replace human activities?*

And yet: Who would want to do without the standard of living; a cell phone, a big house, a car ... nobody.

It *seems* that you can no longer live without all that.

We have probably been in it too deep for too long to limit ourselves only to existing and living.

But shouldn't we at the very least halt any further development at a certain point, so as not to replace ourselves – humanity – in the end? Shouldn't we use our intelligence to save ourselves (and each other) instead of destroying, replacing humans altogether?

Or is it all preordained fate? God's plan?

We crave more, existence alone is not enough for us.
You need appearances and the illusion to not only exist.
Because *existing – after all, anyone can do that.*

Shouldn't we at least prioritize investing our money (as one of many embodiments of misery) in developing and warring countries instead of in the destruction of all of humanity? This way we would finally give money a different meaning, other than evil, **so that one day not only the illusion here and degrading existence elsewhere is possible, but an EXISTENCE becomes possible for EVERY human being, around the world?**
A small monetary donation just before Christmas, while *well-intentioned,* is not sufficient and in this case *not really meaningful anyway.*

In the end, my questions will probably be answered with a "no" up to a "yes and no" or a "maybe", so that our intelligence, despite our stupidity, will kill *us – humankind –* after all. Mass suicide seems to be condoned.
Still, that is one thing we (are allowed to) decide for ourselves.

Does intelligence trump stupidity? Not in this world.

Application

as geriatric nurse or similar

Dear Sir or Madam,

At the outset of my cover letter, I would like to point out that it does not contain any white lies or excuses. I accept the risk of not being hired due to my honesty. However, this is the only way to find out right from the start whether your mission statement and my personality can harmonize with each other, because an employer should also be able to identify with their employees. So, in order to avoid skewing your decision as much as possible, I would like to present you with an honest picture of my personality and the intention behind my application:

I have always been one of those creative minds. Drafting texts has fascinated me from an early age, but my mind was perhaps never focused enough for math and economics.

Particular certainties in life also give a sense of security.
A proper education, for example. After obtaining my advanced technical college entrance qualification, I began training as a social insurance clerk (specializing in general health insurance). It may sound like an interesting profession, possibly because of its interesting name.
Perhaps this profession is actually very interesting for many people. For me, however, it is one of those well-fun-is-then-shifted-into-your-free-time professions; one of those I-definitely-won't-work-myself-to-death-here professions.

After my training, I worked for a few months as a social security clerk in the enforcement department. I then began a dual course program to become a certified financial economist, but I dropped out on my own initiative after four months.

It was the securities (civil service, earnings, etc.) that made this profession tempting at first, but in the end I could not muster the necessary motivation because I completely lacked the required identification of my personality with this profession.

So, I resumed my job as a social insurance clerk – this time at a different health insurance company. The training I had completed in advance had paid off, I could go back to my old job; no unemployment, no more training; just keep earning money.

Day after day, the walk through the endless hallway, past offices with strangers who call themselves colleagues, to the coffee machine and then off to the computer screen. Pressing that start button on the PC is in many ways like simultaneously pressing a button to switch off your brain. I had a hard time doing that, but I learned to pull myself together.

At this point I would like to mention one of my strengths: self-discipline.

After some time, however, I could no longer hide my dissatisfaction and lack of fulfillment from myself. The job and working in a way that was counter to my own personality made me sick. This led to termination of the employment out of self-interest. My former employer is and was not aware of my inner conflict. As a purely precautionary measure, I kept silent in order to continue saving face with colleagues and superiors ... (professionalism).

Since that day, I have been in a kind of self-discovery phase. This was followed by the receipt of unemployment benefits, and also sick pay for some time. In the long run, however, it is not a good feeling to be dependent on the employment agency or a health insurance company. Such dependence also makes finding one-self almost impossible.

Why did you apply as ...?
First and foremost, I want to develop. By working for **and with** people, I hope to learn something about myself, about people in and of themselves, and about society as an alliance of people.
Every person is an individual; every person deserves to be treated with respect.
Unfortunately, as I too have discovered, some people sometimes forget the importance of mutual respect and how it should be taken for granted.
This task will give and teach me respect and appreciation; it will make me appreciate health and life all over again.
This line of work will also help me achieve the financial independence I need, yet it will allow me enough time to continue my self-discovery phase part-time and ultimately it may make me a better person.

The reasons for my application may (also) sound selfish in a curious way, however, the inner fire is the only sustainable drive for any journey – business trips included. You should be literally on fire for any task you can influence yourself.

Apart from a few two- to three-week internships at school (nursing home, kindergarten, occupational therapy, and speech therapy), I have not yet been able to gain any significant experience in this field. A brief on-boarding phase will surely be required, also to overcome any reservations that may arise. Trepidations caused by respect for each person. But therein probably lies the skill: to face a person with respect and be able to help them without actually making them feel in need of help or in any way inferior. A skill that I am fully prepared to learn.

Confused voice recordings

The pioneering confusions that pave the way to more clarity

Deliberately living as a failure

I will make it my personal mission to live the life of a nobody, a failure. The loser that I have long been in people's minds anyway. In the course of my loser life as a person who rejected money and greed, I will limit myself to the minimum. Unfortunately, I do also require a bit of money in order not to perish in this world, yet I will live the life of a typical failure and write about it, so that mankind will understand what it means to live when you can no longer live any other way.

Nobody can become a hero in this world, especially not the nobody who rejects this world. So I guess I'll remain a nobody forever.

Perhaps I will at least become the nobody of nobodies and earn money with this nonsense without further relying on true nonsense like bosses, offices, etc.

Most likely though, I'll just be laughed at again or even ignored. Let's see where this "no experiment" takes me.

Good intentions do lie behind my behavior, because I want to be provocative by being a failure in a certain way. I want to be despised in order to point out exactly this grievance.

Thus, it seems better to me to earn money that I need to survive through my own work, through myself. Then my existence would at least be semi-meaningful – one half existence, one half illusion.

The mask of laziness and stupidity

The mask of laziness and stupidity serves to protect my self, which must not and cannot be here as it is.
Most people will think I am stupid or lazy, but I know: I can do more, but I simply can't anymore.
Everything that seems desirable to others is not desirable to me – on the contrary.

Either it becomes my professional task to point out exactly these grievances and the impracticability of living in a make-believe world, with which I can earn my bread and butter at the same time, or I continue to remain a nothing, a nobody, a failure and earn – like everyone else – my money by doing nothing (as a welfare recipient or the like). Then I can also suck the money out of the taxpayers' pockets – an attempt to destroy money. This possibility would also be compatible (after a long internal discussion) with my conscience.

The third alternative, the fundamental change and improvement of the world, would probably be the least likely consequence of my work.

The maybe-goal

In any case, my goal is *not* to continue living a life of compulsion.
Perhaps my goal is for everything to crumble so that a new beginning becomes possible.
Perhaps I would even like everyone to fail; for each of us to admit that we no longer have any desire for this form of sham life and therefore do nothing but nothing.

Maybe everything has to crumble first, so that a restart becomes feasible, because only in the depths of the sea does one recognize its true beauty, at least how beautiful it can be ... could be.
Is there no love in this world?
Did it ever exist?
Has love lost the fight against hatred forever and have we thus lost ourselves?
Is love merely a craving, a desire in itself, which one tries to realize by all possible means?
Are these means the hatred or do they merely generate hatred?
What are the means? Are they solely financial in nature?
No, it is not just money as the embodiment of greed that is to blame.
Everything is to blame – which brings us back to nothing: Nothing leads to anything, everything ends in nothing.

People will always conjure up sufficient reasons that make change seem impossible.
So, are we lost forever in this nothingness?
Will the something never exist here?

Wearing the mask of laziness and stupidity, at least, seems bearable to me.
At least more bearable than projecting that endless feeling of not being understood to the outside world.
Probably very few people will be able to grasp it, recognize it or accept it to be true: nothingness.
So from now on, I won't just talk about nothingness – I'll embody it.

And regarding that somebody who misinterprets this embodiment because of appearances, I would like to congratulate them with all my heart: That somebody is an inherent part of my own theory about life in nothingness.
So thanks for the unwanted sympathy and proving my theory right that ignoring subjectivity leads to a make-believe world.

The controversial
"giving-a-or-no-fuck-comedy"

Is "giving-a-fuck" exactly what people do without pause?
Giving a fuck, that you yourself and the others, humankind and the world as such ultimately are what they are because we once made them this way?
Does this mean just accepting that and continuing in the same manner?
Just doing it the way it has to be done because there's no other way?
So I'd rather not give a fuck, because it's not like this doesn't affect me so little that I couldn't care less; that I could keep fucking (doing) it.
Does everyone actually give that fuck that I would also like to give if I could?

People seem to give a fuck, the world is just the way it is – so you accept everything as God-given.
Worse – people even make fun of it: buying expensive cars, expensive IT equipment, big mansions, ...
You take what's available.
You take what you can get (in wars).

Whether what you take is right – not a soul seems to worry about that.
Or have people already thought about it, seemingly accepted or ignored the fact that it is the way it is, accepted it (take it), and now make it their own to an extent that, despite the laughter, no longer seems healthy?

Are people even aware of this behavior?
Do people realize that they are performing like a third-rate comedian?
As one of the few non-comedians, I also find it funny somehow, but in a very different way.

Someone once came up with this joke (the modern, money- and remote-controlled life) and the comedians repeat it non-stop, sometimes slightly modified, but in essence always the same; and yet, you still enjoy it.

I do not feel joy because of this living comedy, but rather an inner ridiculousness: the ridiculousness of life.
The ridiculousness of giving-a-fuck-or-no-fuck.
In addition to this feigned joy, I also feel a bit of inner protest.

My protest against the fact that life is merely seen as a joke, that people just go on, that no one recognizes the seriousness of life (its value) – this and our only life – or at least considers it a bit in passing.

Humankind continues to just take it as a fun comedy – you can live a good lie with lots of money, so one believes.
This (mistaken) belief allows them to do reasonably well.

At the same time, you look to experience your own love in other people, even believe that you have found it. It seems that life is even better this way.

Shouldn't life rather serve to search for the "you" or one's own self in order to fully realize it and thus *finally be able to love it* at length, instead of preferring what seems to be otherwise *(the unrealizable sameness)* simply because it is the seemingly only possibility of life/love?

One seems to be too satisfied with this comedy to believe that an honest novel would be better.
Even in an honest novel, you will find a joke here and there.
Yes, even in an honest novel you will laugh, not merely because of the little jokes it contains, but laugh because you are truly in a happy mood – happy with/by/for yourself.
At best, you even reach the "and form": happy with, by, and for yourself.

Even better, this is how you achieve "being."

In the best case, the world, life and being can be connected.
Nothingness would fall away and we would receive a positive
value: love for one another.
Love for what each and every one of us is: a unique being.
Everyone individually. All of us.
Everyone among us.
No one above us.
We.

Is it only the everlasting fall that lets us become unending?
Should we finally start to properly live our punishment's life
for our greed (= the inevitable egoism = subjectivity) *in order* to
become unending?

Do we want *to fall without dying*?
For love? *(The We)*
Would we fall again and again in the case
of the malevolent power?
For love?
Only for love,
never for hatred.
Whoever falls for hatred
DIES.

Hatred always finds a way (a formula) to be. Everywhere.
Even in the world of appearances.
Even in the world of reality.
And also in nothingness.

The question is how we hold it back,
how we give it space merely in our minds,
not in actions.
The answer is: together.

As an honest, real, existing we
with good intention despite/defying greed.
Evil is the deed of (bad) greed.
Life is the greed for goodness.

I would apologize for this long subsequent interpolation now, if it would be a lie, however I judge it to be real (= valuable in subjective terms).

However, one will never be truly happy with oneself in a world for the other, for the others, for compulsion – in a world where those people rule who either have the most money or the most human lives on their conscience.
In a world where it's not love that counts, but only money, and only because it can be counted and measured, and is therefore tangible.
In a world where love does not exist?

Do you just find everything funny all the time, but can't truly laugh? Is that our problem?
Are people fucked worse than they thought, since they gave up long ago?
Everyone will think I have given up, but I have not.

What seems like giving up or failing on the outside is more like rebelling when viewed in my subjectivity.
A rebellion against compulsion.

Sadly, the revolt will probably get lost in the compulsion, so that the revolt isn't one after all – maybe it's actually just a failure.
Have I failed in this world?
I cannot change the world.
In this world, I can't find happiness, but merely the joke that keeps repeating itself.

So I choose, because I can't help it, the no-fucks-given; not for the blanket give-a-fuck.

I don't give a fuck about the fake life and the fake world.

I would lack the necessary drive anyway. Ultimately, I also do not have the necessary job title of "prostitute" (taxpayer, average citizen, role model), to do it anyway for other motives (the love of money / hate) or to suffer it in silence (compulsion).

This world likely translates "not-giving-a-fuck" as failing, doing nothing.

But I'm incapable of everything else. I can't stand anything else long enough.

Compulsion has forced me too much. I can't go back there and I wish it were different myself.

I would love to be one of the comedians myself, because that seems to be one way you can endure it.

Regrettably, I'm not. At times I, too, have taken a shot at being funny, but actually it only served to not be recognized as an enemy (child of reality) in the illusion; in order to distract from all of this, but my mind won't let it go.

I cannot expel it from within me – this revolt, which I can express merely by failing and doing nothing, but which is understood quite wrongly – solely as failure.

Unemployment as an opportunity

I quit my job because I couldn't carry on anymore.

Would it have been better to keep forcing myself to continue?

After all, in my time as a person-existing-in-an-office, my thoughts were mainly preoccupied with getting upset with the other office people – a collection of people, a living nightmare. Working with office people – salaried horror.

So I had my issues there, too.

I could think about these problems all the time: After work they were buzzing around in my head, as well as at night when I dreamed, in the morning when I got up and also after work.

Until they became so unbearable that I ran away from it all.

I never knew why I had these problems. Until now I assumed it was because of myself – that I was the only problem.

Possibly I am a non-human, an inhuman human being and therefore do not fit into any human structure?

Not until I was unemployed did I realize I really didn't fit in there. BECAUSE I am a human being.

Not until I was unemployed did I realize I would never want to go back there, or even be able to. I can no longer force myself to do so.

The compulsion and coercion made me sick, probably irrevocably, but at the same time it also unleashed me, as this compulsion became too binding, so that the forces caused the chains to burst.

Now, in an age of unemployment, I feel I am becoming aware of some things.

Now I can think about life itself and finally be highly in debt.

Unfortunately, I realized that life is, in fact, a joke.

That wasn't my plan originally when I quit my job.

I thought I would manage to find a place in a copywriting agency, or to become professionally active using language in some other way.

But if that means returning to the mills of coercion, I guess I can't do that anymore.

So far, I have not had the strength to apply for a job.

I never managed more than this incomplete draft:

Aborted plan for a cover letter for an advertising agency
(File from 07.30.18)
A structured weekly working time, a job with a secure future, clear task assignments, … MONOTONY!

Most people are probably satisfied with that. You only experience fun in your free time.

For a long time I wrestled with the question: Do I want a secure job, but one that will probably never completely fulfill me and where fun is also more of something you'll receive an official warning for, or do I take the risk of trying something completely different?

On the basis of this text, you will probably conclude: I opted for the risk option. In the end, we all live only once – so why settle for monotony?

I long for a professional activity that I can identify with, that fulfills me and that I enjoy.

As you can see from my CV, I have not completed any suitable training or studies. But is that really necessary? To me, talent and a constant willingness to learn seem like very good prerequisites for advancing from junior copywriter to copywriter. Language and writing have always been a special way for me to reflect myself and others, to inspire, to make people think. Language is always met with an attentive ear, whether it's read …

– End or rather break –

A few months later, I instead applied for a job in geriatric care and other professional care of people.

Not because butt wiping is a lifelong dream of mine, but because I need and want to finally understand people. But at the same time, I also think that there is nothing to understand and thus it will again merely end in an eternal search for nothingness.

Perhaps tomorrow or the day after tomorrow I will think differently again*** and simply go through with the work with and for people. Then I can recognize what I already recognize anyway: The problem lies with people. Not with me. Not with you as the others, but in the person as a person.

If you are the problem and think of yourself and everyone else as the problem, how can you bear this world? As a problem.

*** Yes, I did think differently a few weeks later. I actually started applying for underpaid jobs that "help people."

Hardly any responses followed many applications. One of these was the response from dear Ms. Undank (Ms. "Ingratitude").
I would like to go into more detail here about this application and the response I received, as it is a very specific, ambiguous response (if you know how to interpret it correctly – ambiguously):

Of course: I got a rejection.
It was communicated to me by a woman named Ms. Undank (Ms. Ingratitude).
The irony.
The fate associated with life truly has a sense of humor.

I wonder if Ms. Undank, in her position as an administrative clerk in HR, is exclusively responsible for communicating rejections (= disappointments)?

I wanted to return a piece of humanity into the world of the elderly; at least into their dream world, into which they flee at night when they are fast asleep; but in which they no longer find refuge, because their subconscious has shaped these into a single nightmare since they do still perceive reality.
The dementia patients could be lucky and at least be spared in their dream world; live or dream or even play the role of a human being in it, as they once played as a child, still free from the constraints of the future.
By the way, "thank God" I haven't been able to consciously remember my dreams for a long time. The things I see there must be bad. Almost as bad as the here.

Apparently, this introduction or retraction of humanity is not wanted – that's fine. Ungratefulness is, after all, a pretty form of ignorance.
The irony of fate makes it a truly good joke in the end.
Laughter will help me get over the disappointment, after all, a joke is not to be taken seriously and therefore: not real. Merely a semblance of this illusory world.

At least towards the end of the message they wished me all the best for the future.

That's what I wish for, too. For all of us.

Hope springs eternal, after all: it survives all deaths inside and outside the home.

Thanks for nothing, Ms. Undank.

Sometimes life has to first be completely empty to be filled again with the right things.

If everyone quit their hated job, we could sort ourselves out, limit ourselves to just being and consequently be happy instead of just appear to be happy.

Together, as a world community, decide what the "new world" should look like.

I also expressed many of my thoughts to Ivan.

"I know what you mean, I also get annoyed with a lot of people," was his response. And yet I know: he is annoyed because of his own life story; because of his own self (influenced by others) – because of his subjective view and the conclusions he draws from his own experience.

He's not annoyed for the same reasons, and not to that extent in any case.

So once again I felt misunderstood. I even sensed that he wanted to downplay the problems of the world, while I hadn't even asked for an assessment or his opinion on what I'd said. I certainly hadn't asked about his take on true or false. And yet he went for it.

So he probably did what his self wanted: to justify himself or to provide me some reasons for why I am wrong.

"Yeah, yeah, I know: You're the strong person and I'm the weak one" and "You're not an angel, are you? You're a human too."

So once again I was being made fun of, I was even made out to be a megalomaniac.

While he did say it was all "just a joke," I do think: those were the only statements that, besides his true-false statements, were one hundred percent honest – the honesty that's concealed in a joke; similar to make-believe life.

Or had it in fact been a joke? Does he get me in certain parts?
Perhaps he even did have thoughts similar to mine?
But only he knows that, and I will never find out.
All I could hear was that his thoughts did not reflect my inner self, did not come close to resembling my mentality.

And I was disappointed because of this. I wanted to get away from him as quickly as possible.
Something in me, however, thought this escape was wrong, so I still stayed with him.
That was probably forgiving the otherness.
Your own self may well forgive that someone is different and try to accept that.

But then I did drive back home after some time. He asked why I wouldn't stay a little while longer.
"The real reason will hurt you." But he wanted to know, so I told him the reason: "Like probably every person, I think about myself and my own needs first:
Even though this thing we have does make me happy, it's also torture at the same time.
At some place and some time an agonizing ordeal must come to an end, because you can't take it any longer otherwise."
That torment was occurring within me and due to my self, not because of him.
In an earlier part of the conversation, he had expressed to me that he "sometimes can't carry on any longer because of me."

"I also make the drive because you can't carry on because of me. I, too, sometimes can't go on, but I keep coming back, even though it's a real struggle inside of me every time; a roadblock that I try to steadily fight. This is frequently to no avail, though. Nonetheless, I endure it all again and again, all the time."

I can no longer go through this agony that my inner being is going through – I want to love, but it is difficult for me – maybe I can't, because the mistrust makes everything difficult or even impossible.

Maybe I do love, but it doesn't come to the surface, it's just in my subconscious.
I can often sense it: there's something there. There's more there than just nothing.
Love? Greed? The greed for love (longing)?

After some time, however, agony won out and I felt compelled to leave again: "The fact is: I keep coming back again. And again. And again. And again.
So, in essence, I never really leave, because I merely pass through death, because it's the only thing that keeps me from coming back again and again."
So I left the room, only to enter it again soon.

Every person does everything just for themselves: I keep coming back for me, not for him. I want it that way.

To the extent that he is overwhelmed or "no longer able" to cope with my presence because of what I have said and because of my outward uptightness due to inner turmoil, I do not want to be a drop in the ocean.
Maybe I'd better go. Forever. In order not to harm him.
He should ponder whether and if so, what meaning I have in his life, whether perhaps I might even be doing him more harm than good. He should just think of himself, as one always does anyway, and make a mature decision instead of indirectly accusing me of being exhausting for him.
His problem with himself, which he interprets onto me, is exhausting for him. Not me.

The problem of his inner subjectivity, to interpret my subjectivity accurately.

So I choose the path of being honest about how I feel at all times. I do try to let my thoughts come out into the open, but unfortunately even so they can be completely misunderstood under certain circumstances. Still, I keep trying. It "only" requires strength and effort.

Life and love are hard work; you have to work out a meaning for yourself.

If that does not work, there is still an alternative – "thank the devil" – which is earning money. Here you likely earn what you deserve: no real meaning, just a shiny appearance (of the faces on bills).

Love should not be exhausting, and even if it is, you should gladly accept the effort it takes. Hence it would not be an effort in the real sense, certainly not one that you would have to express or blame someone for.

I believe love can go through both good and bad times, love can start in both good and bad times.

If this is not the case, it probably does not exist after all. True love. Only being honest with oneself can lead a person to happiness.

One can live with deviance, as long as one can accept it. If that's not possible, you should remove it from your life's path.

It's quite similar in your career.

It has to be a source of joy. If that isn't the case: begone with it! Which brings us back to the problem of money.

So at best, money would have to be abolished.

Provided that there are people among us who do their job because they enjoy it, these people will continue to do it even without money; if not, the joy was probably another lie; make-believe joy.

Life is the only something in nothingness that is known to us. The only way to blossom and develop – in the shape of a human being, in the shell of a body.

Maybe everyone lives a different (inner) life, but I am convinced that almost all of us have one thing in common: We are trapped. We can't escape from this cage.
Life in this world is the only known way to experience life without a cage. The body is not a cage, it is the necessary tool for the freedom of our soul.
It is our soul's way of being.

And what did we do? We built ourselves a cage and gave it countless names ("workplace", "community based on solidarity", "presidency", "continent", "mine alone" ...), so no one remembers its real name and meaning anymore.
Did this development really have to happen?
After all, it hasn't corresponded to what really exists for a long time.

At the end of the day, however, man is also a comfortable creature of habit who no longer *wants to (not: cannot) do without certain things in life.*
Have we forgotten how to fly without flying?
Then what's the point of an own soul? Away with it. Chuck it into the trash.

We simply don't know any other way but what we are familiar with. We're simply born into this very cage.
Who would really trade their house for a tent?
Who would even grow grain and such crops, provide for themselves, perhaps even self-sufficiently?
What kind of person would want that? People simply have no interest.
One just has no desire to be anymore. It is no longer enough to just be.

Rather people would like to appear to live a sham life.

Provided we can live further lives beyond planet Earth after all, in those lives, one will probably look back full of remorse on life on Earth. They will recognize only too late that this life/experience was the something in the nothing, the only possibility to blossom and develop, to receive a body that makes acting possible – which allows for you to be.

Yes, people will hate themselves for never having really taken advantage of this opportunity.
But humanity has probably developed into a humanity in appearances.
So I'm not surprised that the first robots are already replacing us today.
Robots as a means of transportation, as a means of food preparation, as a cosmetics item, etc. – everything the false heart desires. Anything to keep up appearances.

One day this pretense and thus the bypassing of being (our destiny) will probably avenge itself on us. *Especially if you believe in higher powers, right?*
When no one is anymore, everyone only feigns an appearance, then people are no longer needed.
Being will die out – humankind will die out.
Simple, complex robots can take over the pretense.
We won't be needed for that (much longer).

That is how I think and feel. But perhaps at times one must accept people who think differently, who feel *(?)* nothing.
However, one should only accept these people provided one can live with the consequences of one's accepting.

You don't have to accept everything, you don't have to see everything as God-given, unless you can reconcile it with your own self; unless no one is harmed, unless no one's being is affected by accepting certain circumstances. *(Asia, Africa, Europe, … all over the world people accept coercion, servitude and modern slavery, war and famine.)*

The gain; the return you will receive because of your acceptance, will it be valuable enough that you are willing to compromise?
The compromise of accepting the other?
This is something that everyone can decide for/with/by themselves.

Despite the coercion, because of which I am not allowed to decide, I will allow myself to decide anyway for once: I opt against this life of appearances and for a life of real existence.
Insofar as there are people who think differently, I must accept these people around me because I cannot banish them. However, I will no longer live a life plan that is alien to me.

Whoever continues to believe this to be right or even necessary for themselves will probably continue to compromise by keeping up pretenses instead of just being. This will be done in order not to perish, because of which those who truly are, die. Day in and day out. Even at night …

I accept that, but I am surprised that this someone is ready to make such a compromise.
After all, even dying has a higher value than upholding pretenses, because, after all, dying is an indication of an earlier existence, or at least an indication of a past, earlier possibility of an existence.
For my part, I will not let my life – as well as I can – be further influenced by the views of make-believe people.

I especially don't want to be left without music, though perhaps I could do without my laptop.
Or perhaps I simply play my own music, and write by hand again?
My own action, carried out by my own hand.

To note down my thoughts, in order to make them part of my self externally as well, physically. Accordingly, this way my self also influences my shell.
A reciprocal effect. An ambiguity. Meaning for the shell.
So I could make my body work for my self.
Through my self. For my own self.

I would make this compromise as long as it allowed for an existence that is unconditional.
But I have to think it over again, because the sense is anyway merely the nothing beside the appearance: The appearance has too great a power for my own decision to lead to an existence for myself – despite and because of the acceptance of thinking differently.

Provided that the meaning is nothingness, why and from where would one muster the strength to create something of one's own? I feel powerless and at the end of my rope, just like many other people. However, nothing impels *me* to work in an office anymore and, as has been mentioned before, it's therefore likely that I am facing a life as a failure; as a wretch, who drains the last few cents from the taxpayers' pockets and, yes, of course: I am therefore that person, who destroys everything. *It's true.*

Pretty confusing, I'll have to consider all of this again.
So I'll probably spend the rest of my life doing just one thing: thinking and pondering.
Looking for a plan that will fail in the end in a make-believe world, for which you probably can't find any willingness to compromise either.

I don't want to accept the deaths and wars of this world, but they will probably never stop. So all that remains for me is the life of a nobody, the life of remorse for the deeds and blindness of people – the life as the scapegoat.

At least it's a life, though, not a make-believe, sham life. Tricky.

I will have to grapple with myself once again.

It does seem unavoidable though: Unfortunately, as a poor wretch I will probably have to accept the strange money of strange people (taxpayers).
Somehow I, too, must be capable of surviving in this world of pretenses. I primarily manage to do so by escaping from the pretenses, and second, by exploiting the illusory world in the form of accepting other people's money.
But hey: I admit my intentions openly.
Whether it's a good or bad decision, the own social status and/or everyone should decide for themselves.

So I will try to create my own little something in nothingness, which unfortunately continues to depend on the illusory world; after all, it is the all-governing power that will continue to inadvertently influence my life negatively.

However, for my "try anyway" I do need some contributions from the dear taxpayers. Or I could use the abolition of taxes and paying with money as a whole.
I would like to apologize for this well-meaning exploitation.
An apology often conceals a small to big lie and an apology for that very lie.
I apologize for living a life of lies, despite trying to be truthful.
I apologize for the nonsensical consideration of this possibility in a sham-governed world.

In a life of exclusive and sincere honesty to oneself, and thus inevitably to all others, also outwardly, yes; only in this way would there be true honesty, true being.
This would also make the apology as such superfluous.
They would not be needed anymore, because honesty is explanation and reason enough.
Being honest with oneself, admitting mistakes, and forgiving – yes, that works without that sanctimonious little word "apology."

You can't absolve yourself of the blame.
You have to live with it (make amends) in order to live.
Only by making amends can we forgive ourselves, not with this one word, nor any other word.

I wonder which someone once designed the idea/concept of appearances and thus deprived people of life through influencing and exploiting thoughts and habits.
Perhaps it was a nobody who had lost their self or never had a tangible self in the first place.
The nobody missed them nevertheless, they missed that something in the nothing, they felt this insatiable and painful longing, which they could never satisfy. So they created the illusion, if simply being was not possible in the first place.

As time went on, they may have found other nobodies who then joined up.
Money, compulsory work, etc. were born and the world became a place where many nobodies lived. These nobodies misinterpreted the meaning, they were too lost to seek their selves.

Over time, some of these nobodies became somebodies again, giving birth to new nobodies. Nobodies who recognize appearances and live a life of punishment through this realization.
A life of insatiable longing – a nobody's life, which is also unsustainable in a world of appearances without the appearance. So these nobodies have to face death day in and day out, but instead of simply dying or killing themselves, they and appearances destroy themselves a little more each day – a long, agonizing death. I absolutely enjoy listening to further accusations from bona fide taxpayers as additional punishment for the actions of nobodies.
I am and remain a good-for-nothing in a world of appearances. Luckily.
On behalf of the historical nobody, as a nobody, I apologize.
This nobody brought a lie into the world.

If only everyone would give up something of themselves to make the world a little better and thus make being possible again one day. After all, I gave up my own self, which I now have to painstakingly find again or recreate.

Other people may have enough money to give away some of it. If the money were distributed equally worldwide, each of us might live in somewhat poor conditions, but then each of us would finally be truly rich: as close to being as we have ever been since the creation of the illusory world.

Ivan

How we met

Our eyes meet. Again and again. Our glances avoid each other. Again and again.

Does love at first sight exist? Or is it rather passion that creates this attraction? I begin to feel that he is watching me.

It makes me feel uneasy, mainly because I can't say for certain what his intentions are.

To be desired – a great feeling. To be desired – an alien feeling. Me, the former fat outsider that I guess I still am on the inside.

No. He's not into me. Surely, he is watching me because of my strange existence, an attraction – like an accident – you can't look away.

My pack of cigarettes is empty. Dammit. I ask the bar patron next to me for a cigarette. Extremely unpleasant, but an addiction is stronger than any sense of shame.

Heavily intoxicated and thus with great effort, he starts to roll me a cigarette. That just makes it all the more unpleasant, but I need a cigarette.

Suddenly, a hand appears next to the drunkard's head, holding a cigarette in my direction. I accept the cigarette, although I can't yet see the face behind.

My subconscious says it can only be the charmer watching me. He bypasses the drunk patron sitting to my left and now stands to my right. His eyes are deep brown, his hair jet black, his beard is neat and also jet black.

A man of depth. A man who understands my longings.

A man of longing.

No. Don't get too carried away, he's a human being like everyone else – mostly devious, but rarely sincere.

My distrust of people *always* manages to make everything look bad. Nevertheless, my interest is strong enough to keep the distrust at bay, but the loud screams still reach my brain, or rather heart, or better yet the part of the brain that is often referred to as the heart as whispered thoughts.

I thank him for the cigarette. He strikes up a conversation, asks for my name and other basic points. His name is Ivan and he has been in Germany for three years. Syria is his home country. Then things fall silent.

Ivan looks to the left and seeks the gaze of his colleague. The latter returns his gaze, smiles and gives him a thumbs-up. Ivan smiles, and I can't help grinning slightly either. He seems to be a little shy.

It seems he doesn't do this often: chat up women.

While it does surprise me, it also makes him much more likable. I almost feel like I know him. Someone who – like me – turns away from the masses and, perhaps in order to seek, searches for the authenticity in life? Maybe.

If it weren't for my mistrust, which makes me doubt my own theory. "As if!" my mistrust screams to my brain in the clutches of my interest in Ivan.

Now I also behave contrary to my habits: I join the conversation and thereby keep it going.

After a few more questions and answers, we grow quiet again, but not in an uncomfortable way. Our eyes are doing the talking now. And the alcohol takes care of our inhibitions.

After countless almost greedy, yet loving glances, his hand slides under the counter, reaching for mine. I'm startled for a moment, then I squeeze his hand lightly but firmly and give him a smile. He smiles back.

We hold hands and continue to gaze into each other's eyes.

This feeling, this situation almost makes me burst.

What is this man doing to me?

"Shall we sit in the back? There we can talk undisturbed," Ivan whispers to me.

Torn, I remain in my seat for a while.

I wonder if he really thinks I'm dumb enough to believe we're just going to talk.

Or is he using "talk" more as a kind of ironic synonym that he knows I will also understand the irony of?

Does he know that I know we're going to kiss and that, despite having this knowledge beforehand, I'm going to accompany him to the back of the bar? Anyway, should this happen on the first night, the night of getting to know each other?

Shouldn't one take more time? Perhaps Ivan is a womanizer after all?

Or does he, too, feel this familiarity that makes taking our time unnecessary?

Although I am still quite unsure, I accompany him.

We take a seat next to each other on a padded bench.

Again he reaches for my hand and searches for my gaze.

When I return his gaze, he begins to kiss me.

His kisses are gentle but passionate ...

Markus

New

A different day, a different time (04:52), a different event, different thoughts from the same person.

Or have I already undergone a personal change since my last day of writing? Perhaps. "Markus New." That's how I saved my ex-boyfriend's new number, without being able to guess at that time in what a sadly ironic way this contact name suited him. Right now he is literally terrorizing me with phone calls.

But up to this point, a lot had happened beforehand.

He was my first great love. For the first time in my life someone made me feel so much – after years of being mocked because of my tendency to be overweight and an outsider per se – a desirable woman; despite or with or even because (?) of my flaws. Quite early on, the phase began when we seemed to hate each other more than we loved each other. He had a tendency to lie (effortlessly even while maintaining long eye contact), he seemed to hardly have a conscience, a total know-it-all, and in a way bossy.

If you love a person with all your heart, you often love only the image you have of that person. But do we really know who that someone is? Don't our own thoughts automatically make someone a stranger to us?

And really, aren't we all but strangers to each other, because everyone passes through an entirely different world of ideas and no one would comprehend what the other really thinks and feels in the process of using words? Is there really the perfect lid for every pot, or do we simply construct our own lids and pots?

How you see yourself, how others see someone, and who you are – three different ways of spotlighting a personality.

How often do married people cheat, involving people you would never have expected? How often do seemingly balanced people kill other fellow human beings in the most cold-blooded way? How often have people done things that we would never have believed them capable of when viewed from the outside?

You can literally only look at and not inside a person's head.

But I digress.

In my ex-boyfriend I saw my savior in the face of adversity, my hero, a brave and self-sacrificing man. Even if he raised his hand against me once, I still saw that in him. Or wanted to see it.

Surely, I could not have been so mistaken about a person?

A series of incidents – mostly lies and the resulting jealousy and distrust – made our relationship as tenacious as chewing gum. It no longer gave me wings, but I couldn't live without it.

I had never really managed to get along quite well in life (especially in terms of interpersonal relationships) and finally I had found something to hold on to.

Alas, I held onto someone who seemed to have long since lost respect for me.

But the main thing was that I could hold onto something.

We ended up quarreling over every little thing.

He preferred pleasuring himself on the toilet rather than with the once so desirable woman. I also noticed some competition in a woman from a lingerie ad. In my eyes, all he still lusted after was women's bodies.

Which was, of course, an exaggeration and led to untold drama.

At some point he started to leave.

And I started chasing after him.

I often spent the night alone in our shared apartment after he once more ended everything at the end of an argument.

I was floored every time – how could I live without him?

After all, he had helped me in every situation that life threw at me.

Yes, he was also opinionated and domineering – but I got over that, because when you love, you compromise.

But I should never have made one compromise: to forget myself for someone. I would have done anything for this person,

I would have forgiven anything for this person, and this very person began to say his farewells. Not only once. Again and again. And yes – it also felt like that every time, because each time, I could never know beforehand whether I wouldn't lose the fight for him.

In the end I did lose him. And the fight as well.

Or maybe I gave up voluntarily because I just couldn't carry on anymore?

I had defined my whole existence only by "us", I lived for us: loved, laughed and cried far too much. Everything revolved around us. Our problems mostly. Or my problems, but they also had "us" as a possible cause. As mentioned at the start, he probably loved me also because of my flaws, that is, my low self-esteem.

For what proud woman, what proud man would allow themselves to be treated this way?

I often wondered if he actually understood the cruel thoughts and feelings his actions triggered in me, both in the short and the long term. On the one hand, there was this incredibly strong feeling, which to this day I don't know if it was love or simply the longing for a vastness inside me. Sometimes, this yearning is so agonizing that I just wish I had already arrived.

On the other hand, it was an extreme dependence on this person. Too often I had left my chores in his hands.

I had forgotten how to do the chores of (daily) life on my own and thus I did not see any possible solution without him.

To me, he was the solution to my problems and at the same time he became a problem because these problems turned into a drama about my ego because of us. When our relationship began, I didn't know who I was. During our relationship I was (also in my eyes) Markus' girlfriend, and after our relationship I had lost myself.

The phase of self-discovery would probably have begun much earlier had I not successfully suppressed this phase for years.

For me it was easier and nicer to define myself as part of a couple than to think about myself and my ideas about how to live. Maybe because I knew that I could remain alone with my ideas.

And because I was afraid of being alone. Because being alone permits thoughts to emerge that maybe I didn't want to allow. However, I would have had to allow them to become who I am. Now I am in my mid-twenties in this life and ask myself, what was the sense of my entire past and who even am I. Above all, I wonder how I should now fill the remaining years of my life to make them meaningful for me – how are you supposed to know that if you don't even know what you actually want, let alone who you are. Since then, everything feels somehow numb and alien.

I still feel like I haven't quite (re)arrived in my old childhood room, and that's after half a year including renovations.

Probably because I never really wanted to go back – never take a step back in life (from independence back to "Hotel Mommy"), but also never a step back into my past, which was filled with bad feelings.

I was incredibly afraid of the moment of "moving back in."

On the inside, I was already preparing myself for nights full of tears.

I knew what thoughts and feelings scared me: In every crumb I would recognize him and be painfully reminded of the loss of him and of my new (now old) world.

In my old (now new) world, everything would remind me of my past.

Above all there was the fear of meaninglessness and the fear of my agonizing longing for something indefinable – I call it vastness, that sums it up best. But that feeling didn't materialize – apart from a few strange flashbacks. It's living with no particular direction. My old world had become a different, new world. A new world that somehow feels alien. Alien or maybe just not right, I don't know. For a young person without the financial means, sometimes your parent's home is the only accommodation option that remains, sadly.

I probably wouldn't feel any different in my own apartment: Everything feels empty and pointless, but above all somehow alienating.

Unfortunately, I have no idea whatsoever where I would feel at home and what circumstances might give me a sense of security and familiarity (with myself – not self-confidence, but that's probably included).

I want to create something of my own with my life.

But to do that, I first have to figure out what makes me into something of my own.

It was precisely in this phase of self-confusion that a second chance for Markus and me loomed. It began with clearing out our last shared apartment. That's where we met again for the first time in about four months.

At the end of the day, he took me in his arms and sounded so remorseful and insightful.

He said he missed me every day.

Above all, this day ended for me with a sense of triumph.

Again and again I chased after him. I never thought these words would be possible, coming from his mouth and especially not at this time.

I had accepted my new life in the meantime, or rather I just get up every morning for reasons that are still inexplicable to me and get through the day without really living it, because I lack that sense of life. Life = Being = Freedom = Happiness.

Yes, I think there is that feeling and I just don't have it.

Once I finally feel that sensation, I know life will be easy.

Easy, no matter how difficult the circumstances may ever be.

After that shared day in the old apartment, we decided to keep in touch. No more, but (sadly?) also no less.

I was aware that this would make it almost impossible to let go of the world as a couple and maybe that was exactly my hope: that there was still hope for an "us."

A few text messages eventually turned into meet-ups for a few intimate hours. These hours were full of passion and at the same time familiarity and above all pleasure. The non-committal nature of it all with a person I was once bound to – positively tied to – made it thrilling.

Thrilling perhaps also because it secretly reinforced my hope that there was a chance for another us.

A few more meet-ups followed and at some point he began to use his domineering and commanding manner sexually as well. Text messages like "Send me a nude pic of you, that's a precondition for meeting up again", "I can give you money for a new car – you can pay it off or you can earn it", etc. made me distance myself again for the time being.

No more meet-ups followed and that felt better.

I did not want to become dependent again – even if only sexually – and feel that I had to be obedient in some way for the closeness and affection of a person.

During this time I met Ivan – and decided to get to know him better.

However, Markus (remarkably) did not give up. Again and again he wanted to meet up, again and again I refused. Until the day that initially left me incapable of making decisions. We talked about getting together with good prospects for a shared future. The possibility of trying again – someday, maybe.

So there I was with the choice between a new partnership and thus a new risk or the old partnership.

With a partner who had to actually love me.

He already knows me inside out (or so I thought) *and still wants me back*: I could be certain *he loves ME and not the version of me that's only seen through rose-tinted glasses*. Markus wanted to help me after I told him in confidence about my current situation (unemployed, on sick leave, struggling financially, ...). At first, I was grateful, but then a growing sense of being oppressed crept back in.

I realized that during the time I was alone, a power had matured in me (despite not knowing myself). This strength gave me the necessary pride to talk back. Markus, however, was unfamiliar with this coming from me. He said to me that I had changed.

In the end, I found that he, too, had changed.

Not his circumstances or his way of speaking, but HE.

I desperately searched for my Markus, but there was a stranger standing in front of me.

One night that was bursting with thoughts, I realized this and it turned into a night bursting with tears. A second farewell to Markus, but this time forever, because I could not find him anymore – he was as though dead to me. Not "dead to me" out of anger, but actually gone and no longer someone I could grasp.

With that came the certainty that I had a choice of living a lie or embarking on a journey into the unknown.

I decided on the latter and informed Markus of my decision.

Since then he talks about further friendly meet-ups and still offers me his "help." Sometimes I think that's his (way too extreme) way of showing sympathy or even love.

But I now know that this kind of love makes you sick.

Plus, I want to manage my life using my own strength and not through the pressure of an outside force.

A letter

to the best friend

Dear Best-Friend-Soul,

I was actually looking for the Winnie the Pooh for you and was even more disappointed when I couldn't find him. You said that you also had a stuffed bear in your childhood and that's why it would be great to have this one. So my plan was actually to treat you to it. In hindsight, however, I'm glad I didn't find the bear. I mean why copy a stuffed animal from the past (childhood), if there is also the option to give you stuffed animal(s), to which you will say in a few years as an adult, then even more mature than you already are (mature in the sense of mentally mature): That's what my best friend gave me back then – it was a great time, sometimes the world annoyed us a bit, but we could give each other comfort, curse at all the crap together and the most important thing: we could laugh together. Laugh, even if the current circumstances in life for both of us are or were not in fact a laughing matter. There is nothing more valuable than people who – no matter when and how – manage to put a smile on someone's face.

Sometimes I regret that we didn't become such good friends much earlier.
You give me strength – simply by the presence of your great character.
So I hope all the more that in a few years the stuffed animals will not only be a symbol for the memory of me and our friendship.

I still want to be your Bratan even as a (probably bitter) grandma.
At least in my heart of hearts you will always be my Bratan, no matter if we fight – because we make up again afterwards.
No matter if we ignore each other – because sooner or later one of us always reaches out again.
No matter that we are somehow different – because that's how we complement each other.

In my eyes, you are a very strong character. Of course I have seen your tears, experienced you in situations where everything seemed quite pointless to you.
Nevertheless, a person who manages to make suffering people feel better, even though they themselves are suffering, is a person of incredibly strong character.
It is in any case a sign of strength to be able to cry, and above all: to cry in front of another person. I'm glad you cry in front of me and that I can also do so in front of you.
I don't need friends with whom I can and may only be strong. For me, a best friend is enough, to whom I can show all of myself without fear of being rejected or not being seen.

In the meantime, I've come to a point where I can say: No one knows me as well as you do. No one knows as much about me as you do. And no one accepts me like you do.
You wouldn't believe how much strength you give me – even without giving me specific advice or help; simply because you exist in my life. I'm grateful that you asked to see me. Someone who every now and then pulls me out of a (my) monotonous life and allows me to feel a certain sense of freedom. It feels good to be able to talk to you.
But what does fucking wonders for me: Turning up the music in the car and just singing along – no matter if you hit all the notes. Feeling music lyrics, recreating melodies and forgetting the inner tensions for a moment – that somehow gives me a feeling of freedom.

I can't be like that with ANYONE but you: just letting it all go, not worrying if it'll be weird if I screech more than sing a song. Because I know: If you know the lyrics, you will join in and if you don't: You just let me sing. You just let me be – be me.

Other people would become so annoyed at some point and probably shout, "Now shut up!" But not us. And that, to me, is one of the greatest things in life.

I still don't know exactly who I am or what I want from this life, but one thing I do know is that I want you to always be a part of my life because that's what you are: a part of me. It may sound a bit over the top, but you are my spontaneity, my craziness, my letting go, my belief in better times ... Yes, because of you I have regained all of that and it's a great feeling.

Our friendship will always stand above everything else for me. Even if it may not seem that way at times in the future. You know how I sometimes slip into relationship things, maybe even have a tendency to get emotionally dependent quickly.

But this is exactly the crucial point: You are not part of my life because I want to appeal to you and am looking for safety and security with you.

You are part of my life, because with you I am – quite automatically – the best version of myself or rather because you give me the chance to become that (and this is my own best version, not the generally socially accepted or even demanded best version).

Because you just take me as I am. Be it euphoric, happy, bitchy, naive, ...

Inwardly, I hope you feel the same way about me. I know you have a much larger circle of friends and know more people than I do (I doubt I even have such a circle) ... Nevertheless, I hope that I am also a special person to you. But I am – for a change – confident enough to say: I think I am.

After all, you call me Bratan and that's not something you just throw around!

After all this talk about God and creation, I would like to finish by saying a few words about your present:

As I mentioned before, you are an incredibly strong character in my eyes.
Strong as a lioness. No. Much stronger. A lioness with a unicorn. With a glitter unicorn.
But even lionesses cry. Actually, that's precisely what makes up a lioness: To feel pain and be able to feel and yet to have that inner strength and never lose that inner glow.

If you ever don't feel well, I want to be there for you. And if I'm not physically near you, I'd like to be at least mentally (hence the baby comforter, which at least has a cute bear head, even if it's not Winnie the Pooh).
Sometimes there are setbacks in life and no matter how hard something may ever knock you down, no matter how deep the grief, no matter how hopeless a situation may be:
You are never alone.

Never lose faith in yourself – I will always believe in you.
Faith is the wrong word. Know. I want you to know that you are amazing, because I (and many other people too) already know it for a fact.
You are amazing because you are you. Not because of any formal education, not because of any material possessions, not because of your coolness (although we are already damn cool, uncool and I more than love us for it).
You are Mandy. And that's perfectly enough to be amazing.
Even back in the day, I knew you were a cool person with a great sense of humor.
But today I know that you are a lioness.

Thank you for everything you give me – a lot even unknowingly or unintentionally. I look forward to more years of spontaneity but also being laid back, of stupid decisions but also smart conclusions, of hours of (seemingly pointless) conversations but also gaining mental maturity, of craziness but also returning to sanity and feeling like there's someone who just goes along with "all this shit" …

At times as a silent and supportive companion, at times as part of a two-person team, but always as a friend.

And it's become clear to me:
I do have a huge circle of friends.
1000 friends in a single person.
1000 qualities in the character of a single person, of which far too many people do not even possess one quality.

Maybe we still haven't found true love (or shut our eyes to it). What we have already found, however, is true friendship – **we are rich**.

Surprise, this poem is titled "Sometimes"
No. The title is:

Sometimes all it takes is the presence of a very good friend

Sometimes I don't know how to carry on,
but you still cheer me up again.

Sometimes an inner longing almost eats me up,
then we just turn the music up loud.

Sometimes I don't want to see other people,
but I know that I can always go to you.

Sometimes I hate myself and my quirks,
but you will never expect perfection from me.

Sometimes, when I'm in an especially bad way,
I can feel my heart begging for a friend.

Sometimes my heart wants to discover the vastness of the world,
then we drive somewhere – regardless of whether that's with
or without a check-in.

Sometimes, in quiet moments, I realize:
Our friendship gives me back a bit of vitality.

Sometimes I wish that
I might be equally important to you.

Sometimes the time has just come to say:
I really cherish you and I am so happy to have you.

Although we are different and often disagree, I always feel like
there is someone who somehow gets me. Getting someone does

not mean having the same views. To get someone means ... to understand someone.

Yes. To simply understand someone. Maybe because you already know them very well.

Perhaps because, despite all the differences and quirks, you have found a friendly kindred spirit ...

Thank you and please,

yours in deepest friendship,

Sandra

Conclusion

The Presumption of the Existence of Love

It requires the acceptance of the other, of subjectivity and thus the awareness that no one thinks, feels or even is like oneself, which does not result in *being* alone, but probably rather "*being* self-aware."

However, this acceptance is not to be realized by adapting to each other, but by truly accepting. True acceptance is not easy for anyone, yet it is the only promising way to genuinely love.

The result of this awareness is sincere honesty towards the other person; after all, another person can never feel like you, think like you or be like you.

Is there just the adage "a lid for every pot", or are we all just human pans after all?

Only those who genuinely love sincerely feel *loved themselves*.

Whether the other person (the maybe-you) genuinely loves, only they know.

So you can only trust (not believe) that the other person also accepts the other and is therefore honest. Can you be mindful of love?

In case of the love of one's self, in order to achieve this, one should recognize and get to know oneself, to ultimately know oneself best. Only that person who is aware of their self and its value can forgive their own mistakes and thus accept themselves. If a person manages to accept themselves with all their faults, they will manage to be honest with others with ease, because they can't be any other way – only honest. Honesty is something that every human is capable of, but which only very few implement as a long-term concept in life, although it could replace almost everything in life.

For it is not appearance that is valuable, but being, or being able and allowed to be.

So is love just the acceptance of the different?

Yes, that is all it is. It is what is hardest for all of us; that which was missing one day and was replaced by appearances.

Love is being as us. The merging of two selves into one "We", without the respective self ever being suppressed or disappearing.

Love reigns where simply being is allowed.

If everyone loves themselves, everyone in this world will be loved. That's a fact.

The love of another can only be questioned when in doubt, and the honesty of the answer, the honesty of the other to their self, can be trusted.

But where does this trust come from in a world of appearances? That's probably where my distrust of love comes from.

To be able to trust in spite of the endless mistrust requires a lot of courage. It seems to me that this courage is almost impossible to muster. Yet if you truly love a person, you will muster that courage; even in this world.

You can create love yourself.

Whether one has lived a lie in the end and thus not truly loved and lived, only the other person knows, but one knows oneself: One had the courage to love.

According to legend, good things happen to brave people, and according to my legend, lying people earn a lot of money.

Just a joke from the margin of society.

Deceitful people pay with the loss of their own selves, that should be punishment enough; after all, they led a life of pretense.

Nevertheless, there is also Evil in this world, which is not afraid of punishment or is not yet aware of it. Ignorance does not protect you from punishment.

You can sense, even without knowing, whether your actions are right or wrong; whether your actions are harmful to yourself and others.

The lie makes loving and being a sham, for both or all parties respectively.

Accepting one's mistakes and expressing them to others leads to two possibilities:

1. the loss of a false love or false friendship.
2. the bliss of true love or friendship.

Because love does not demand happiness. Either it does or does not exist.
The mere illusion is equal to a lie and therefore does not truly exist.
Those who love can forgive. He who truly loves only makes forgivable mistakes; thus, does not constantly commit acts of deceit, does not use physical violence (hatred is easy to detect, even through an outward appearance), etc.
Hate is easy to spot, but difficult to fight.
That requires the courage of every good person to love in order to eliminate hatred and evil together.
A somebody alone can't do this, a nobody probably can't either.
A last spark of hope does not let my thought, my assumption of the good in people, die out.
That's probably why I became a nobody, or already was after leaving the birth canal.
No one but me seems to have any hope left, it seems to me.
I don't know whether that's truly the case. Appearances have always blinded me; if they remain, I myself will probably perish from my own hope, which has become a disappointment. So far, I have not yet been able to glean any real being from an illusion, so of course I cannot know whether the Good or the good Evil is in the majority. But one may safely assume so. Although assume is the wrong term, I exclusively assume evil, but feel the good outnumber the bad.
Unfortunately, it seems to me, feelings can also be deceived by appearances.

So the question arises whether one can actually love oneself.
You could in a world beyond appearances.
Should my feeling be correct, the result will be that the good will act.
If it is not right, I will probably always remain this nobody.
Has anyone ever loved? Is it possible to love? Has anyone ever been loved for who they are?
Once a rigid doubt exists, nothing (except nothingness) in this world still has meaning.

We will probably never know how much love is actually waiting for us. We will only vaguely guess at it, only sense it within us, as this unsatisfied longing.
Instead, we would rather invest this longing in the appearance of love.
It is very difficult for me to love. I don't know if I even can love. I don't know if *anyone* can anymore ever since Evil took over.
Otherwise, would the power of Evil have ever been allowed in? Otherwise, wouldn't one finally fight Evil?
I don't know, but my subjective guess is that is the case.
As is revealed to me once more: Unemployment and a certain distance from Evil form the only way to hear the inner self (the self that exists in me after all?).
After all: it exists.
Sometimes it still scares me too, in my eyes there is nothing worse than a soul that is truly ill.
But gradually, even young people are starting to realize in their own subjective way: ill is not just ill. Unemployed is not the same as unemployed.
Good Evil exists. The illusory Good can only be Evil, the illusory Evil is also Evil in reality, because minus still results in minus. The equation is also valid in language (human actions).

In a world of Evil, the true faith is: faith in love.
After all, one can only guess at it, probably never know about it, because what is disguised as love is never a synonym, not the definition or even the proof of love.

Unless you find the proof within yourself.

Those were *my* closing remarks on love.

My end *of* love.

My beginning *of my love*?

PS: Maybe-you gave me a glittery-shiny-beautiful watch at the beginning of the shiny-beautiful-simultaneously-horrible romance. **His** interpretation of the *language of language*: "It just takes time"? Or has language long **since** *spoken* to us: "It's about time!"?

The language is difficult to understand, it is muffled by appearances.

Anyone who allows their own thoughts to form can hear and sense them: ***The speech/language of language.***

The distance to love –

out of love or all out of love?

Excerpts from a digital conversation on the day following the assumption of love:

Me: What time do you have to leave tomorrow?

You: About 2 or 3 pm.

Me: And for how long exactly?

You: I think until Thursday.
(You're starting a new job including installation work.)

Me: Okay, I *want* to be honest with you. It may hurt you, but *not as much* as *you* hurt *me* yesterday (not deliberately). But I *am* hurt. *I feel* offended and therefore do not want to see you for the time being.
But my intention is a *good one*, even if you don't see it.
Having said that, I do love you very much.
What *you* believe and think about this, you'll have to *decide* for yourself.

You: What do you mean by that?

Me: I don't want to have to keep repeating myself just *because* you *never* really listen.
The whole last conversation, especially the end, *was insulting* to me.

You: Yesterday I said that I *know* you are writing a book.

I only thought that that's not the *whole* story behind your absence. It *wasn't* an insult.

But what *I quite honestly* would like to tell you: I *am* quite certain that you no longer want *me. That's* why you're "purposefully" *doing* all this, just to get rid of *me*. But that's totally fine. If you no longer want me, then just *say* so. *Just* say it.

Me: Do you also read the "to me" when I write to you that it "was an insult to me?" But what it was for you – I don't have a clue. In any case, it hurt me (nevertheless). Sorry for being honest.

You: I only said that was not the real reason for your behavior. I never said I thought your book idea was ridiculous.
Obviously, I'm happy you're enjoying it.
But I just thought that was not the truth.

Me: Well yeah, I still want you and that's exactly why I can't see you right now. I don't think you'll ever understand that. Just as I sometimes don't get you.
Sometimes you have to accept that the other person is different and thinks differently. So you compromise. True love is a compromise.
That's how I see it, you seem to view things differently.

You: (voice message)
I don't understand why we are arguing right now. What about? I never said anything about your book – I just wanted to know the truth. So you told me you are writing a book. At first, I didn't believe you, then you wrote … What did you write again? I forget. Yes, you did: You wrote again that it's the only truth and then that was it for me.
I promised you that I wouldn't say a thing about your work, as you wanted me to do so you could finally tell me about it.
I replied that if you tell me the truth, I will not say anything about the truth.
And that's what I did. I just didn't think it was the truth.

Man, I'm really mad at you now. Really pissed off. (loud voice) (further voice message)
I didn't mean it that way and you always think badly of me. Always. Always!
And I don't want to hurt you or anything.
You know, friends of mine wanted to come over today because I'll soon be gone for several days and I canceled everything because I actually wanted to see you. But not anymore. I do not want to see you today.
(in the background you can hear a loud knock at the door and a voice calling)

Me: You don't take my work seriously enough. Not seriously enough to take it as "the truth." I am the work, I'm my own therapist, the others can't do it, I write down my thoughts, maybe in the end it will turn into a book – Need I say more?
You didn't take my work seriously, but it's my only refuge, SO OF COURSE IT'S THE TRUTH.
You think my work is – and by extension – I am a lie, that can't be the (only) reason for my absence in your eyes. Think about it. Please. I believe exactly right, but apparently no one else believes correctly anymore.
For a few days now I have been believing in myself a little bit again and then you come along, calling it a lie, me – a lie. Go a little further with your thoughts. Don't just stick to the surface. I am mad.

You: (voice message, another voice can be heard intermittently in the background)
I got all of that. But I said NOTHING about your book.
The only thing I said was that it's probably not the truth, there must be something else behind it. If you are writing a book, that's normal, totally normal.
But YOU are doing all this ESPECIALLY because you want to get even somehow or get rid of me because you are afraid you won't be able to stand my absence.

THAT's what YOU mean.

Me: It was clear to me that you would think that way. Too bad.
My thoughts are quite different from yours.
Do you hear me? Completely different. Maybe TOO different
for you.
You always only see Evil in me and behind all my statements,
I only want Good and that is why I am honest. Only by being
honest with you can I continue to be with you. Now I'll be hon-
est and say:
I can't see you now because you hurt me and don't understand me
or misunderstand me all the time. But: I do want you. Forever.
That's what "I love you" means. Even you said so, and I think so too.

You: Why are you hurt? What did I do? What I said yesterday
I think is quite normal, I didn't say anything about your book.
Absolutely nothing.
Just that it couldn't be the truth. You said, "Yes, it is," and I re-
plied, "Okay."

Me: You thought my book, my work, the search for my ego was
a lie. You thought there was actually something else behind my
behavior.
This is not the case, but what I said, instead.
Why can't you see the insult in this? It's so obvious.

You: (voice message)
Nooo, no. I just thought there was something else. I didn't say your
book itself was a lie. I believe you, that you are writing a book.
Of course I'm glad if this makes you happy or if you enjoy it.
Like I said, I just thought it was not the real reason for your be-
havior.
So what do you want right now?
Sorry if I hurt you. Sorry, but I didn't mean it that way.

Me: Are your colleagues there yet?

You: Yeees, just one though. But don't worry, he doesn't speak German.

Me: YOU are the only liar between the two of us.
Sorry, but you won't be able to reach me for a few days.

You: *(two annoyed emojis)* Bye.
– *End of the conversation* –

My assumptions about my keeping my distance:

Primarily, I am mostly just disappointed because my not-yet-a-book, and that in a sense, myself, is seen as a lie, or at least not a sufficient enough reason for a full-time occupation.
However, *I was occupied* full time because of the writing, *because* of the searching.
A person who already considers themselves a "nobody" is doubly affected by such words. *What's it like for other people? I don't know.*

Ultimately, I just *wanted to* prove something to myself, I wanted to find or at least create my self *without* any external influence.
Now, *however*, he's aware of my plan because I opened up to *him* that one time.
I myself can think *of no greater* influence than *that of* a lie; *the* accusation of not existing. Like *a* nobody. Simply *without* the shell. Just *like* the illusion.

Second, I'm disappointed because *I've* been accused of lying about it.

And third, I'm disappointed because this *very* person *who is suspicious of me is lying too. Lying to* me. The one I already told *from the very beginning*: "Honesty is the most important thing for me", demanded it as a *condition* for becoming a couple.
He said yes. *Probably only for appearances?*
The one who *always stressed* and still stresses this importance.

Again and again. The one who often *(enough?)* showed her honesty by openly admitting mistakes she's made. But also by *answering* what her inner self *says*; what she *subjectively thinks* when asked *"What are you thinking right now?" "What have you been up to?"* But also when it comes to seemingly trivial things like *"Do you love me?"*

Is love the betrayal to the self?
In a way, I feel betrayed and cheated out of myself.
My own fault? Should I never have let him in this deep?
Because he can understand it completely wrong, namely different-ly than the I?

I wonder if he even wanted to see me at all?
There it is again. The *doubting of* everything. The *knowledge of* nothing. And *the anger.*

If you are *truly* disappointed, you need distance instead of close-ness.
Closeness makes *closeness* worse, since after all, *anything* the other person could say or *do* can only *seem* false; only *feel* like more lying and simultaneous mistrust. At least subjectively speaking. To me.

The question of whether one *can* forgive and accept *can* only *be* settled with *oneself or at least figured out – the inner question. Sadly, however, people don't have a remote control for their selves. Or do they?*
Is the external one-appearance this remote control? The faith in ob-jectivity?
Personally, I don't believe in it.
I *have* to deal with my thoughts in order to become, to be one.
That's why I didn't want to see him for the time being.

The question whether one can forgive someone's *disre-gard* of the self and the *simultaneous* **question whether**

"one's own self" is *actually* disregarded *by* the other person can likewise *only* be answered by oneself. That's to say *at least* as far as one can judge this *"self"* and do so *subjectively – so really, actually not at all.*

You *can only* make *(= act) out* of that what you yourself *want to see in it.*

No one is honest all the time.

And so, for the time being, **I want to see, hear or read nothing that's connected to him. Nothing.**

But the Maybe-You *merely* sees the lie, the pastime in a perpetually striving, honest person?

Has humankind long since recognized the lie, the illusion, sees it in everything and hence resorts to lying as the only possible response?

My main idea / original intention: The distance is also necessary to, at least for a moment, freeze any potentially real but not provable true love instead of destroying it using words full of anger. But people have always preferred to grab a weapon.

As always: This is my subjective opinion.

Whether this still remains my opinion now – I don't know yet. I need some space first.

Hopefully Maybe-You still had a great last night with his friends.

Yes – I mean that honestly and seriously and strictly as I said.

As a fourth point, and not to be forgotten, I am disappointed because I told him about the pressure building up inside me as soon as *even just one further* person knows about my work before it is finished. Before I could decide for myself whether it was good or bad. This pressure probably also arises because the Maybe-You means a lot to me and this meaning forces me to create a significant, but at least good "life's work." Nevertheless, I told him about it because I thought I could trust him.

Trust that he has truly heard my subjective fears that I had already expressed. And that he considers these as much as possible in his subjectivity.

He did not judge the process of writing a book.

He "only" devalued it.

In order that I could still work on it, to lend *my book and myself (Us? You?)* some worth again, even if it was but a little. *That's also why* I felt compelled to distance myself from sham love or "maybe-love."

From selfishness, to become and remain true to my emerging self.

Reasons

After the end of my story, which is probably at the same time the beginning of my own story regardless of its outcome, I would now like to mention the reasons that prompted the story.

It all began one night when I was sitting alone on the old two-seater leather sofa amidst the chaos of my cold, dark bedroom, losing myself (the actual chaos) in someone else's music. Anonymously, I wrote the following YouTube comment about a German musician.

This artist wears a mask to protect his identity, so that not mentioning his pseudonym seems the right thing to do.

Perhaps some someone will read between the lines and be able to recognize the musician in question. I think a person must probably accept this eventuality despite the mask; people ultimately expect an answer to everything (the nothing).

At the same time I ask myself which masked musicians will feel (falsely) addressed; who will see or look for their I in another You. This type of false search was also the intention of my own YouTube comment, which I deleted after two days.

Fortunately, my remark had not yet been evaluated, commented on or judged/condemned.

After all, it was a message to myself to finally look for the I within myself. A message to my self that was not meant to reach ANYONE but myself.

Not to be read, understood, and judged by anyone but myself.

So I considered it the beginning of my search, but I did not condemn it; not even to this day.

YouTube comment:

"I am almost ashamed of myself, since I've only discovered 'Pseud-onym' now, but I will continue to listen to his music despite every-thing, as the closeness to a kindred soul feels extremely familiar. It's quite possible I may sound like one of countless groupies, perhaps I'm nothing more than that in truth.

Perhaps, however, this post is merely the expression of my joy at having found a person with a possibly similar mindset (and thus a seemingly similar view of *the* world). Quite comfy in 'his base-ment' – I could definitely hang out here for a while to relax ... "

The most important thing – also in my world – in closing:

Friendship – the nearly-what-love-in-this-world-would-have-wanted-to-become-connection

Friendship resembles an almost-love. At least if the friend is a true friend.

My best friend appears to me as a true friend.

"Appears to me" is not meant to mean that this friend acts or tries to impact my own self. Quite the contrary.

After all, "appears" is the opposite of "seems" and therefore "acts." This friend acts like a friend to me through his actions: Lan-guage and actions, whereby actions, arguably, fundamentally have the higher value in my world, because words should not be trusted too much – you can bend and break them.

Perhaps he does affect one's self: the true friend.

But if that is true, it is the only person who can do it without altering the self at its core. You know the saying "You make me a better person."

Consequently, friendship would be approximately equal to lan-guage in terms of its value.

Sounds like a great concept for a (my) world.

This friend is totally different from me.

He appears extroverted, self-confident, and mostly life-affirm-ing despite having phases riddled with doubt. In all honesty, I admit that this obvious otherness *was annoying at first.*

We would often talk about topics such as love, jealousy, fears, dreams, and goals, or merely the choice of dinner.

It turned out that this friend was not just a "yes-man" but has his own ideas about life, his own self.

That was the effect of their appearance.

As a result, the one or other conversation turned into more of a heated discussion about the right way to look at things.

But there is no such thing as one perspective; objectivity.

At the end of the discussions we usually said things like: "Then I must have misunderstood you", "I'm sorry about that" and more rarely "I never thought of it that way – thanks for pointing that out."

Naturally there were days when we had nothing to say to each other.

Even days when we ignored each other, because both probably sensed it subconsciously: this space is necessary.

After this period of time, during which each of us was probably preoccupied with our selves and our thoughts, one of the two always reached out again. Again and again.

Nothing but honesty – consistently.

We accept each other as we are. At least that's how it strikes me. I can be who I am at my friend's side: namely, as I want to be at this moment. He gave me the feeling that our beings were coming closer, converging.

Acceptance of the different embodies true friendship.

Whether my best friend thinks similarly of me, I don't know, but I don't care.

Because it will not (and should not) affect my subjective view of this friend.

Is there anything more than a something in nothing?

So far, I've found friendship and language. Maybe more is hiding behind all the appearances in this world. I am curious to see what else will come to light and whether one day it will come to this: being.

"Let me know when you're available again."

Note from my "almost-self":
*Dear friend, I **will**.*
*You'll be the first to **know**.*
*Because what is **truly important** belongs at the beginning;*
*in **life**, not (only) at the end, the ...*

*... **Hey you**? Hello? **It's me**. Hi.*

*Friendship lasts a lifetime, because true friendship **is** for life.*
So what are we going to do about love and appearances?
*Shall we let it ... **be**? (Warning: sexually-untouched double entendre)*

Peek

into another book

Hello. My name is Sandra.

This book is about my search for salvation.

I had already written a book, but then I burned it.

It was a book about God and Creation; I managed to explain the world and God and their origin in a new, different way.

The result was a severe psychosis, although I still find some of it to be very real today.

The end of the story: I thought I was God.

Now I hope everything will go back to normal – I want to become the old Sandra I was before I started questioning everything.

I have always been rather introverted and felt a deep longing inside of me.

Perhaps the longing for true love.

At the same time, I'm very shy around people and not very self-confident, so I do often get in my own way.

A five-year relationship was followed by a few male acquaintances and another six-month relationship. He ended that when the disease began. He claimed to be "not ready for a relationship at the moment." He seems to have deleted my number by now, though occasionally he still visits my profile on an online dating platform.

What I was left with was my family, and it's never really smooth sailing with them. And yet I am glad to have them, they visited me regularly and cared for me. They never let me down.

From February to July 2019, I was in a psychiatric ward: first in a closed ward, then in an open ward, again in the closed ward, and finally back in the open ward.

Writing has always given me pleasure and at the same time made me sick (my first complete book).

However, despite everything, I don't want to give up my passion. After all, it's the only thing I know how to do – at least a little bit – and also one of the few things that bring me joy.

Among other things, occupational therapy was offered in the psychiatric clinic, but I am not very adept, nor am I a skilled painter or good at sketching.

Writing is my passion.

My first book was supposed to be (or rather was) my life's work, but unfortunately I burned it in the hope it would make me feel better. I did not.

The psychosis got worse, I suffered a great deal, and a lot of it seemed very real – maybe a part of it was.

But I don't want to deal with this question any further (at least I am trying to gain some distance). I want to look forward and somehow try to lead a normal life again. I do hope that the writing process will help me do that.

After elementary school I attended high school. From the third to the ninth grade I was overweight and was bullied a lot – that's probably where my low self-esteem comes from. It also doesn't automatically rebuild itself when losing a few pounds.

I still feel that I'm a bit too fat.

My body is full of scars, in part due to stretch marks and also because of my self-harming behavior throughout my school years.

I was always quiet and just took whatever happened to me.

In the past, I often wanted revenge, but now I have more important things to worry about: myself.

After completing high school, I obtained my college entrance qualification and trained as a social insurance clerk at a health insurance company.

I had no idea about this profession, just applied because it sounded alright.

After completing my training, I worked for a few months at a health insurance company located a few miles from home.

A short time later, I started a dual study program at the tax office, but soon realized that it wasn't the right fit.

So I dropped out of college and started working for another health insurance company.

After a few months, I couldn't keep kidding myself: This drab office job with set instructions didn't fulfill me.

So I quit without having anything else lined up. Instead I wrote my first book, which ultimately brought me a lot of misery: I was unemployed and incapable of working. On top of that, my driver's license was revoked because I made "a confused overall impression" (the onset of psychosis).

To regain my driver's license, I have to take a psych exam which I have to pay for out my own pocket.

So I've hit rock bottom, even though my plan was a completely different one: to find something that fulfills me.

But maybe one day I will be able to achieve this after all.

I often feel very lonely.

Although I have my family and my best friend, there is always this feeling/thought: "Nobody understands me", "Nobody thinks like me", "Nobody feels like me".

Everything merely scratches the surface. You only experience real depth – in conversations, for example – on very rare occasions.

Boredom quickly tempts you to start thinking about things.

Either about God and Creation, the world or about your own life.

My ex-boyfriend calls my behavior "sloppy" and thinks my search for love is an excuse.

That's actually pretty hurtful.

In addition, a few weeks ago I wrote him that I will likely love him forever.

I wanted him back, but he has a new girlfriend by now.

And yet he was not averse to the idea. But then he made me wait and wait and did not end things with this woman.

Made me wait too long, so I started to open up again a bit for others.

I met a young man and after a few meet-ups we also slept together. Being the honest soul I am, I told my ex-boyfriend this and the result was a barrage of insults, that I had become cheap and sloppy, that I had lost control of my life.

Perhaps I had.
Perhaps my search for love is merely a sign of pure desperation. I often feel very lonely. I long for a partner who is just as submerged as I am; pensive, melancholic, full of longing, …
But most of the time everything just scratches the surface and yes, it's true: Most men probably "only want one thing" above all. But why give up hope and the search?
I don't know. My loneliness literally forces me to keep on searching.

I spent the weekends during my psychiatric stay at home at my parents' house.
My life seemed to return to normal – a strange feeling.
At the same time there is this hope that everything stays/will become normal and this fear that it (the psychosis) could start all over again.
My wish is simply to live a normal life again: live at home, go to work, etc. – just stand on my own two feet again and not be ripped out of life like that.

So now my life is slowly returning back to normal and I'm looking back on an experience that I don't quite know how to deal with (yet). It's just unfathomable what happened to me.
Whether it was real or not; I can't forget it, I carry it around with me, it has negatively changed my attitude towards life. As mentioned before, there is this near-constant fear that something strange could happen again and at the same time it (still) feels strange that nothing strange happens anymore.
Nevertheless, that does make me happy and I do hope it stays that way. Now my task is to learn to live (freely) again.

Social anxiety

and binge eating

In the meantime, it has been a year since my therapy at the clinic. I haven't written in a long time, lacking both ideas and the necessary drive.

But now I want to pursue my passion again, document my search for salvation once more.

It began during the daily morning circle: everyone has to briefly share how they are feeling and what plans they have for the day. The first person started to share and I became more nervous with each subsequent person.

My heart started racing, I felt dizzy, and I began to tremble.

It became so bad that I had to leave the circle without saying anything.

Not only that, these problems also crept up in the smoking area, so I started avoiding that as well.

I've always been quite shy, couldn't stand lectures at school and so on.

But it has only been this bad since my psychosis.

What was I afraid of? Why am I so afraid?

Was it the bullying at school? A long-term effect?

I don't know, but what I do know: you can't live a happy life like that.

I decided to go and work for a health insurance company again.

Looking back, the job may be a bit stale, but it's also interesting and ultimately my only way to earn money again.

I don't feel ready for college (yet): meeting new people, integrating, ...

That just scares me too much and I am sure I would be an outsider once again.

My old boss has promised me a job, I could start in February/March 2021 (after my medical-psych exam for my driver's license). Now it's September 2020.

It seems easier to go back to an old job than towards an uncertain future (college) full of social challenges.

So now I have a few months to recover further and deal with my social anxiety.

I've already had a first consultation with a therapist, "So why are you here today?"

"Because of my social anxiety and binge eating."

"How does the social anxiety express itself?"

I mentioned the morning circle and the fact that I can't go shopping by myself. Bus and train rides are terrifying for me as well.

"Tell me something that is going well in your life."

"I get along really well with my sister."

"Does she know about your problems?" "Yes."

"And your parents, too?" "No."

My parents would just worry unnecessarily, ask questions, and maybe even question the diagnosis. They'd say that perhaps I'm just shy.

"How does the binge eating manifest itself, how much do you eat?"

"A bag of chips, a bar of chocolate, two slices of cake, several pieces of toast; just about anything I can get my hands on."

"Which one do you think you can get a grip on faster?"

"The eating."

"Ah, OK. Why is that?"

"Well, I think the eating can be managed with discipline. The social anxiety, on the other hand, is a fear that is deeply rooted in me."

"And what do you envision? Creating a meal plan?"

"Yeah, that would be a good idea."

"You should ask yourself what you want to do instead of eating. Maybe try consciously eating an apple.

Do you have any specific skills? If your mother were sitting here now, what would she say you are good at?"

"Writing poetry or composing lyrics."

"Ah nice. Perhaps, instead of eating, you could write about a young woman who describes her road to recovery."

"That's a good idea."

So the therapist gave me the encouragement I needed to write again – about my life, my phobia, my eating disorder, friendships, and love.

I think I gorge myself on food to block out my feelings of being alone.

Sometimes, maybe just because I'm bored.

I am currently unemployed and so have a lot of time on my hands. Too much time. Time in which I am often alone.

Every now and then I meet up with an old friend who I only recently reconnected with.

The new

old friendship

Lisa and I were best friends in our teenage years.
The first boyfriend, the first cigarette, the first beer up to the first alcohol poisoning – we experienced all of this and much more together.
We were inseparable.
Until a man destroyed our friendship.
She had seen him before me, warned me about him, apparently he was a bit strange.
She said he had followed her in his car and so forth.
Still, I met with this man.
I thought he was great, so I became involved with him.
I didn't believe my best friend, or I didn't want to believe her.
We broke off contact with each other because of this.
A few years later, Lisa wrote me, "Hey, I know you don't want to hear from me anymore, but please give me a chance to explain myself just this once."
I ignored her message.
Nearly ten years after our friendship, I was longing for true friendship.
My previous best friend was now taken and during my time at the clinic she found a new best friend.
So she only had time for me now and then.
Today our relationship is a bit distant, at least from my side.
I am even quite nervous around her due to my social anxieties.
So she has become more or less a stranger to me.
But due to this longing, I wrote to Lisa: "Hey, how are you? I'm sorry I didn't respond at the time."
She got back to me and we made plans to meet up.

Several meetings followed and she noticed that I had become very quiet.

One evening, an argument broke out.

She had invited me over to her place and I showed. However, I left after a short time.

What followed was this exchange of text messages:

"No offense, but what the hell is wrong with you?

You want to come so badly, then you're here, but you don't say a word the entire time.

And such a short time it was on top of that.

I really don't know what to make of it.

If you don't feel comfortable in our company, why come at all?

I really don't mean to be mean, but I just don't get it and it doesn't make me feel good either.

I or rather we [she and her boyfriend] just want to understand. We were looking forward to the evening and then you left so early, with me thinking what are we doing wrong that you don't like our company."

"No, it's all right, I'm always this quiet, I'm sorry, but after the psychosis I've changed quite a bit."

"Sandra, seriously, that is not the only reason.

Especially since this is the second time you left so early.

It really comes across like you don't feel like doing this, even though you asked me if you could come over.

Even when we are alone, you only say the bare minimum. With this guy [I was seeing a guy regularly] you seem to feel more comfortable staying over at his place every Saturday and not being gone so early.

Do you get what I'm saying?

We tried to include you and make you feel safe, so you'd feel comfortable. But apparently that's not enough.

I think it's a real shame and so does Max [her boyfriend], by the way."

"I'm just as quiet with that guy ... If you can't handle it and it bothers you that much, then okay, I guess I'll have to accept it."

"It's not that it's bothering me. It's killing me to see you like this.

133

Don't you understand? You were my best friend, we laughed non-stop.

I adored your laugh so much, in particular.
But now, not even your laughter is genuine anymore.
We understood each other without having to say a word.
Now I don't even understand you WHEN you say something, because everything is somehow so cold and without emotion."
"And what do you want me to do about it? It hurts to be like this, but I can't just up and change it or I would."
"The old Sandra isn't gone. She shines through often enough. But you don't allow it. And that's what hurts me.
You don't hold back and sing along to 'Alter Mann' by Knorkator, have a hell of a good time, and when you notice that the old Sandra is coming through, you shut her down.
Notice anything?"
"Yeah, but it's not like I'm doing it on purpose. I can't control it."
I didn't get a reply after that. There was just silence for two days.
I updated my status with the song "Join me" by HIM, to which she responded "great song."
She also said we needed to talk and that she wanted to help.
I told her that I wasn't sure whether she could even help me.
She replied that if I wanted it, then yes.

After this confrontation I cried for the first time in a very long time.
It pained me to hear that I had seemed cold and emotionless and that she even thought my smile was false.
What kind of person had I become?
When we finally met again, Lisa expressed the assumption that I might have changed so much because of the medication I still had to take.
The report regarding the approval for my driver's license also described that I exhibited a "Parkinson's-like appearance." Something that may have been linked to my medication.
I think it was a combination of both: my phobia and the medication.

My phobia often makes me tense up and I surely look the part. On the evening in question, there were four people present. Because of this, my phobia got the upper hand and I completely tensed up, both on the inside and outside.

I didn't say a word or maybe a sentence at most.

After a while, I could no longer stand the state I was in, so I had to leave.

The unwanted

friendship-plus

As briefly mentioned earlier, I was seeing a man for a while.
I met him on an online dating portal.
For two months we just wrote to each other, we got along so
well that he started writing "I ... you" without us ever having
seen each other.
I was afraid to meet because I thought I was too fat and because
of my phobia.
So I kept delaying and dragging it out further and further until we did finally meet.
We went for a walk.
Nothing else happened, nor did anything happen on three fur-
ther dates.
At the fourth date, he asked if he could kiss me. I said yes.
The next time we met, I spent the night at his place, we drank
some alcohol, and we also had sex.
This was followed by a few meet-ups where we would do something: We drove to Münster, went out for a meal once (luckily
we sat next to each other, so there was hardly any eye contact,
which makes me nervous) or we went for a stroll by the lake.
This was followed by meet-ups where we merely drank and slept
together.
He also made a few statements that hurt me quite a bit.
After seeing me naked for the first time, he texted me the next
day, "If you want to lose weight, you have to exercise, walking
is not enough."
When we were watching a music video that featured women in
bikinis, he said, "You used to be that skinny."

Following those statements, I felt even more uncomfortable than before. Being naked was especially rough for me.

After some time I realized that no feelings were developing, and I could not forget those hurtful words.

I thought he didn't like me the way I was.

He always said he didn't mean it, that he didn't think I was fat. But I couldn't believe him.

So I finally ended this short relationship.

Now I am single again and I think I will focus on myself for now.

The strange
ex-boyfriend

I was always in contact with my ex-boyfriend Markus, sometimes more, sometimes less.
When I was still in the clinic, I wrote to him that I will probably always love him.
He had a girlfriend and so nothing came of it.

After I ended the relationship I just described, we met up. We went for a walk and slept together.
After that, I asked him more often if he was free.

"It's going to be a late one tonight," "I'm having a barbecue at the lake tonight." were only some of the excuses he'd give me for not having any time.

At some point, the whole thing pissed me off. Enough for me to write to him: "Well, I think we're going to drop 'us', chasing after you has become too dumb. And besides, I'm not just out for sex, unlike you. I can't take your praising words about me having been such a good girlfriend seriously either. Have fun and have a nice life."

To which he replied, "What else are you after?"
"We'll see what comes of it."
"It was just supposed to be based on sex. A break from the daily grind."
"I'm not interested in that."
"If you're really serious, take out your copper coil."

I think he likes the idea that I might get pregnant.

He also wrote me recently that two buddies would be coming over at the weekend and asked me if I'd like to come over for a threesome or a foursome.

I declined. "What's wrong with him?" asked Lisa when I told her.

I have no idea. Start a relationship with him?

The thought now seems strange to me, so I will probably stay single for the time being.

EIN HERZ FÜR AUTOREN A HEART FOR AUTHORS À L'ÉCOUTE DES AUTEURS MIA ΚΑΡΔΙΑ ΓΙΑ ΣΥΓΓ
 HJÄRTA FÖR FÖRFATTARE UN CORAZÓN POR LOS AUTORES YAZARLARIMIZA GÖNÜL VERELIM SZ
CUORE PER AUTORI ET HJERTE FOR FORFATTERE EEN HART VOOR SCHRIJVERS TEMOS OS AUT
POINKÉRT SERCE DLA AUTORÓW EIN HERZ FÜR AUTOREN A HEART FOR AUTHORS À L'ÉCOU
ΒΣΑΙΖΛΟ ВСЕЙ ДУШОЙ К АВТОРАМ ETT HJÄRTA FÖR FÖRFATTARE Á LA ESCUCHA DE LOS AUTO
TEURS MIA ΚΑΡΔΙΑ ΓΙΑ ΣΥΓΓΡΑΦΕΙΣ UN CUORE PER AUTORI ET HJERTE FOR FORFATTERE EEN
ARIMIZA GÖNÜL VERELIM POINKÉRT SERCE DLA AUTORÓW EIN HERZ FÜ
SCHRIJVERS ВСЕЙ ДУШОЙ К АВТОРАМ ETT HJÄRTA FÖ

The author

Sandra Sievers, born in 1995 in Stadtlohn,
Germany, grew up with her parents and two
siblings in her family home in North Rhine-
Westphalia. After elementary and secondary
school, she completed her specialized
baccalaureate in the field of "Health and Social
Services" and trained as a social insurance
specialist. After a few years of working in the
insurance sector, she was struck with the illness
which is inextricably linked with her first book.
Today she is receiving therapeutic treatment.
Outside of her work as a writer, Sandra Sievers
enjoys spending time with friends or looking for
inspiration and relaxation on long walks. Music
also plays a special role in her life, which – as
mentioned in the book – she ideally expresses by
loudly singing along in the car.

> *He who stops*
> *getting better*
> *stops being good.*

This is the motto of novum publishing, and our focus
is on finding new manuscripts, publishing them and
offering long-term support to the authors.
Our publishing house was founded in 1997, and since
then it has become THE expert for new authors and
has won numerous awards.

Our editorial team will peruse each manuscript
within a few weeks free of charge and without
obligation.

You will find more information about
novum publishing and our books on the internet:

w w w . n o v u m p u b l i s h i n g . c o m